Chloe's Enchanted Attic

Jerry J Yeaman

Chapter 1

Chloe opened her eyes to the dim light of early morning. Tragically, she knew that today and all of the days to follow were tumultuously altered. She was not in her own room, but in that of her Aunt and Uncles' spare room, after having been whisked there last night. Some unspeakable fate had befallen her parents while they were away on a hiking trip and she was at home with a guardian. The door was ajar and she heard the muffled whispers of her Aunt Meg and Uncle Jim from the hall way;

"I'm heartbroken; I wish that she could stay here…at least for the summer."

"I as well, but she will be well looked after at Grandma Jens. She is a little eccentric, but I'm sure a comforting host in this trying time for Chloe."

"I agree, and I also think that large old house in the country will be a good distraction for her."

As she lay in bed, she pulled the covers over her head. Her cheeks felt wet from a nights' worth of crying. Her body felt numb. Her whole world had been turned upside down in the space of a few hours. What was to become of the rest of her life? Who was her family now? Suddenly she felt very alone in the world...impossibly small and inconsequential.

Then, befitting her penchant for spunky resolve, she threw away the covers and stood up. Looking around the room, she went to the vanity table and peered into the mirror. Horrifyingly, she didn't quite recognize the figure staring back at her. It was herself all right, but somehow her perception of her own identity seemed changed. Certainly the same eleven year old girl stared back at her.

She saw the same short red hair with its' characteristic disheveled tuft sticking up on top, that freckled little nose, and those large knowing blue eyes. But she seemed to now be a different person...someone else. Her dad, William, always called her 'little spunky', as she had always shown a sense of sure footedness and plucky demeanor. Those things now seemed to be somehow missing.

Looking out the window she saw that it was now a bright, early summer morning. So bright as to seemingly expose anything that was hidden...even that which may want to hide. She felt the latter would be her...wanting to hide from everything and everyone including herself.

She dressed quickly...nervously...and went downstairs. The smell of bacon and scrambled eggs greeted her upon entering the kitchen. Her Auntie Meg and Uncle Jim looked up at her from their breakfast and her Aunt said;

"Good morning Chloe, I hope that you were able to get some sleep. Your Uncle Jim and I are very sorry for what has happened. Please come and sit down, I'll get a plate for you." She walked over and sat down. After Auntie Meg brought her the plate, she couldn't fathom actually eating any of it and just fiddled in it with her fork.

Uncle Jim watched her and said;

"Your' Auntie Meg and I really wish that you could stay here for a while, but we have some pressing business that we have to attend to. The family feels it is best if at least for now that you stay with your Grandma Jen." Auntie Meg added;

"We know that you haven't seen her in a very long time, or even if you can remember her at all, but she is eager to see you and have you stay with her." Uncle Jim interjected;

"We will take you there after breakfast. It's quite a long drive to get there, maybe six hours, as it is in Oregon. We both think that you will get along there well enough for the summer. Grandma Jen is a family favorite...a very kind and interesting person. When your' Grandpa Jack was still with us, they travelled quite frequently, as he was an ambassador to India."

As promised, the car ride was lengthy. Chloe watched out the window as California suburbs faded away and the dry landscapes of asphalt and grassy hills became more mountainous with trees. She did at least sleep in fits and starts throughout the trip, and felt herself quite awake when they finally turned off of the highway. The surroundings were very lush with evergreen trees, large ferns, boulders and mountains. They travelled along a two lane road for a time; then turned right onto a very small road...possibly a driveway. It wound up steeply around more trees and ferns. The afternoon light filtered faintly through the high branches, casting an eerie glow all reflective of green hues.

They then came to a plateau and she saw a very large Victorian style house sitting in the middle of a forest. It was painted in blues and greens with yellow trim around the many wood framed windows. There looked to be a solitary third story room perched on top with a steep pitched shingled roof. It had French doors with yellow curtains that were opened onto a quaint balcony. Opposite the house on the other side of the circular driveway was a barn complete with a hayloft...though it looked unused.

They drove around the graveled driveway and came to a halt in front of the house. A large black cat sitting on a cushioned bench on the front porch gave them an unwary stare. Just then the heavy wooden screen door opened and out came who Chloe could only surmise was her Grandma Jen. She didn't really remember her, as it had been a long time ago that she had seen her. Her only memory of her was that she had long dark hair and seemed tall. Grandma Jen waved at them as some silver bangles on her right arm clinked gleamingly.

"Hello...hello!" she said to them in a light cheerful voice, followed by an infectious giggle. She wore an interesting burnt sienna colored cotton dress. And she had on dark eye makeup that worked well for her. Chloe thought that she didn't look like a typical grandma... she liked her very much. She suddenly felt very uncharacteristically shy. Her present state of affairs were making her feel closed off and guarded, she hoped that it wouldn't reflect badly on her now as she exited the car to greet her.

Grandma Jen gave them all a hug as they stood near the car, exclaiming;

"I'm so happy to see you all!" Aunt Meg replied;

"We're glad to see you too...I just wish it were under happier circumstances..." Grandma Jen said;

"Oh my, Chloe...you do have much of your dad in you with your pretty red hair. I understand if you're not feeling yourself right now so don't worry about being especially cordial right now." Chloe was feeling sheepish and shy as she hugged her. She liked her perfume, and the strong hug that she got. She was usually quite a talkative little girl, but her grandma was right...she couldn't get a word out right now.

"Let me take your bag," her grandma said, as she led them up the steps and onto the front porch. Chloe again noticed the black cat still sitting there on the bench...it seemed to be giving her a disdainful look.

"Don't pay Rowena any mind Chloe, she's a temperamental old thing," Grandma Jen said to her, as she led them into the house.

They went through the foyer and towards the kitchen. Chloe looked over her shoulder into the rest of the house. She saw a wooden staircase leading upstairs, an expansive antique rug covering the wood floor of the living room, a large fireplace, and many pieces of antique furniture. Chloe heard the screen door slam and saw Rowena dart around and run into the kitchen with them.

"Everyone please have a seat...take a load off," Grandma Jen motioned as she set Chloe's suitcase down. The kitchen was well lit by a large window beyond the table, which overlooked the driveway. The three of them sat down as Grandma Jen busied herself making some tea. Chloe stared out the window into the forest. She felt herself daydreaming for a while and not paying any attention to the kitchen conversation.

Just then, some movement along the floor near the doorway to the foyer caught her eye. Her mouth dropped open...a mouse was standing there upon its' hind legs and was facing her...on one supporting leg with the other crossed, and one outstretched arm with the palm of its paw bracing itself upon the door jamb...leaning there as a human would! And was it really looking her straight in the eye? Then, to her creeping astonishment, it winked at her with a mischievous look on its' little face! Just then, Rowena turned her head from her water bowl...hissed at it, and chased after it into the foyer and up the stairs, disappearing around its' bend.

Chloe looked at the others in the kitchen...there was not any break in their conversation, as they hadn't noticed any of it. Had she imagined it? It had happened so fast...and it was just so strange. She couldn't imagine saying anything to them about it; especially since she hadn't said a thing since she had been there...they would think she was crazy. She then started to doubt her own sanity, or maybe the stress of her situation was playing tricks on her mind just now. Auntie Meg looked at her, continuing;

"We were just talking about your Grandpa Jack. As an ambassador to India he knew many important people there... and here as well." Grandma Jen countered;

"He sometimes also took me there along with him, and we lived there off and on over the years that he held that position. I met so many fascinating people, including the Maharaja himself. He was said to have a harem of beautiful princesses all to himself."

"Once, we were invited to a feast at his palace. All of the regional royalty were there, dressed in their finest clothes...men with silk turbans of bold colors...women with painted eyes, henna tattoos, and jeweled necklaces. Truly, it was captivating to me. And the Maharaja Rajeem was entrancing to behold, even from across the very long table where we sat. I remember feeling transfixed by his gaze anytime his eyes settled upon me. He wore a midnight blue turban of shimmering silk with a large, most incredible amethyst colored jewel set in it...it seemed to radiate its' own eerie sparkling light from within."

"And he had large black penetrating eyes under bushy black eyebrows, and a thick matching beard that came to a slight, curved point." Uncle Jim asked;

"Didn't Grandpa Jack's assignment come to some unforeseen and abrupt end?"

"Yes it did, I was living here at the time while Jack was finishing his last assignment there…it was scheduled to end in a few months. Then there was some kind of media blackout…no news was coming out of there for weeks and I was frantic with worry."

"Then to my surprise, one morning I awoke and Jack was sleeping beside me. I was so relieved, yet mystified at the same time. I couldn't imagine how he had gotten there, as I was told by our government that he should have still been in India at that time. Then unusually, he slept for days. He only arose for short times to eat and shower, then crumple exhaustedly back into bed. I was very worried and getting ready to have the doctor come here when he finally snapped out of it."

"Later, whenever I queried him about what had happened over there, and of the other mysteries that were left unanswered by him, he would get this far off look in his eyes and I could tell that he would start to feel sick and exhausted again like before…so unfortunately, I had to let myself be left in the dark about it."

"Sadly, he was never again the same person. He would frequently toss and turn in bed at night. What nightmares plagued his mind I could not guess, as he also muttered incomprehensibly in his sleep. Sometimes I would become very frightened when I could make it out, something about;"

"The eyes are watching… he's coming… leave me alone!"

"He also rarely left the house, he seemed almost frightened to. He was always checking the locks on the doors and windows. As the few years that he was still with us went by, he started to relax a little…but only a little."

"Oh yes, and most unusual of all, it seemed that I was also being affected by his being tormented as well. At night as I lay there next to him during his fits, I would think that I was hearing things elsewhere in the house…noises like things moving around…and different kinds of voices. It was terrifying, and I wasn't sure if I was more afraid of the noises, or of the feeling that I was losing a grip on my own sanity."

Chloe watched her Grandmas' face as she spoke. That last point about feeling a loss of her sanity hit home to Chloe. Hadn't she just felt the same after seeing that mouse wink at her? She thought; "I'm only eleven years old…and I'm feeling so lost and ill right now. I wish she wasn't telling me these strange and disturbing stories." Suddenly, the prospect of staying in this house became unnerving. She wanted to go home…but she had no home now to go to. She pulled her feet up onto the chair and hugged her knees.

Uncle Jim stood up, saying;

"Well, unfortunately for us two, we have to turn right around and head back home tonight. Our schedule won't allow us to delay." They all rose from their chairs, and her aunt and uncle hugged her.

"We leave you in good hands Chloe. We love you, and I know things will be ok for you here for the time being," her Aunt Meg said. Chloe stayed behind and watched out the window as Grandma Jen waved goodbye while the car receded down the driveway.

The screen door then slammed and Grandma Jen came around the corner. She said;

"I'm sorry Chloe…I hope I didn't frighten you with all of my silly stories. Sometimes I can get carried away. Well, let's take your bag upstairs to your room, shall we?" She took Chloe's hand and suitcase and led her upstairs. Upon exiting the stairway on the second floor, Chloe looked up at a solitary wooden door that stood slightly ajar at the top of the stairway on the third floor. Grandma Jen noticed her looking up at it.

"That's the only room on the third floor, it's the attic. There's nothing too special in there, just some old furniture and bric-a-brac. Feel free to explore in there if you wish, there are no rooms that are off limits to you my little angel. My bedroom is there at the end of the hall. If at any time during the night you feel that you need me, please don't hesitate to come see me."

She opened the door that was directly opposite the stairway, continuing;

"This will be your room while you're here. I hope you like it. It has a lovely view of the woods out front." They walked in and sure enough, one couldn't help but notice the large window with a spectacular view of the sun setting over the forest, framed by floor length curtains of pastel mint green. There was an overstuffed brass bed with a matching green comforter and a worn teddy bear sitting atop. A blush rose colored area rug covered the center of the wood floor at the foot of the bed. The walls were painted a lovely shade of pastel violet.

She couldn't help but feel cheered in this nice room, she liked it very much. She then finally found her voice and exclaimed;

"Thank you grandma, I love it!" She smilingly looked up at her as her grandma said;

"Oh Chloe, please feel at home here. I do so hope that you can feel some comfort here with me in this time that we have together."

She knelt on both knees and gave her a big hug. Immediately Chloe felt her eyes burst with tears…she hugged her grandma tightly.

"My little angel…my little angel," her grandma said, as she stroked her hair. "Everything will turn out all right for you, I'm sure of it. Please don't ever feel alone, as I will always now be here for you." Chloe felt reassured and loved…and truly grateful. Her grandma then rose to her feet and said;

"Your Auntie Meg said that you had already eaten before you arrived, but if you get hungry during the night, you can always find something in the kitchen. There are oatmeal and raisin cookies that I made today in the cookie jar on the counter, please try some." She turned to leave the room, looked back and said;

"The bathroom is at the other end of the hall, and there is also another one down stairs. I'm going to take a bath now, and then go to bed. I spend a lot of time at night reading in my room, so don't feel that I've disappeared if I get carried away with my nose in a book. I leave my door open, so come say hello any time that you want company."

"Ok," Chloe answered, as her grandma ventured off to take her bath.

Chloe turned and walked to the window. The sun had set over the trees but it was still dusk. There was a large tree with thick boughs just outside within arms' reach. She slid the window vertically open and cranked a handle which opened the framed screen outwards. The large bough was within stepping distance…she wondered if anyone had ever stepped onto it. It was so large around and there were some other sturdy branches to hold onto.

She noticed that the water had stopped running in the bathroom, and heard as her grandma slipped herself into the tub. She looked back at the tree…it was beckoning her to step onto it. With a semblance of her old self returning, she stepped out of the window and onto the bough. She didn't feel the least bit frightened as she looked down, as it was such a sturdy tree with so much room for her to sit. She held onto a thick branch and sat with her legs dangling over the side.

It was still nice and warm outside, and the air had a nice fragrance of jasmine. She saw Rowena looking up at her from the ground below for a few moments, and then continued her walk towards the barn. The air was thick with the sound of chirping crickets, and she also thought that she heard bull frogs belching in the distance near some babbling brook. It had gotten dark now, and she was surprised at how brightly the stars shone here in the country away from any city lights.

Just then a shooting star arced across the sky and her eyes quickly followed it from right to left. When her eyes came to rest upon the innards of the tree, she was shocked to see that no more than a few feet away was an opossum hanging upside down from its tail, and it was staring at her! Initially, it gave her quite a start and she gripped a branch for support. But as soon as she realized that it was not agitated at all of her presence, she again relaxed. Feeling a bit silly of mood, she spoke to it;

"Well, hello there Mr. Opossum, shame on you for giving me such a fright. Don't you know that it's not polite to stare?" And then incredibly, it answered her in a perfect British accent;

"So sorry, I'm Mr. Oppum…and who might you be?" Chloe's face contorted in horror, accompanied with a stifled scream.

The shock jarred her from her roost and dislodged her little body from where it sat. Luckily, she was still gripping tightly to the branch as she dangled perilously over the edge of the bough. She hoisted herself back up, and without looking back at the animal, jumped back into the room. She slammed the window shut and ran to the bed, grabbed the teddy bear, and dove under the covers.

"What is happening to me?" she thought. "I must be going mad…first the mouse…and now that opossum!" Never in her short life had she felt so afraid. This was all too much. With her eyes tightly shut and her body nervously shivering, she felt like she was in shock.

After lying there for a little while, she heard her grandma open the bathroom door and walk to hers.

"Are you asleep my angel?" Chloe feigned sleep. She just wanted this whole nightmare to go away. Maybe if she could just quickly fall asleep, she would wake up tomorrow in her own bed, and all of this would only have been a bad dream.

"Good night," her grandma said, as she switched off the light and walked away to her room. Chloe lay there for a while as frightening images of all the recent events flickered through her mind. Eventually, she drifted off to a troubled sleep.

Chapter 2

Chloe awoke to the loud clanging of a pan hitting the floor from the kitchen down stairs. She heard her grandma otherwise lightly bustling around, most likely making them both something to eat. She did at least get a good night's sleep between some troubled patches of strange dreams. And no... yesterday's events were not all a bad dream, hence here she still was. The teddy bear was still clutched in her arms.

She got up and went to the window. It was a beautifully clear morning, although still quite early, as the sun hadn't yet risen above the trees. She looked over to where she had seen that nightmarish creature...and of course now it was nowhere to be seen. It had to have been an imagining of hers, as there was no other explanation. Well, she didn't want to linger on these thoughts... she was already tormented by them all night in her dreams. She decided a hot shower, and a clean change of clothes, would wash away all of these troubled cobwebs in her mind.

Later, she did indeed feel much better as she made her way down stairs to the kitchen. The wafting smell of pancakes with maple syrup, bacon, and coffee was a mesmerizing siren.

"Well good morning my angel," her grams said, as she noticed Chloe standing in the doorway of the kitchen.

"Good morning grandma," she answered, as she sat at the table. "Did you have a good night's sleep?"

"Yes, thank you," she answered, and then queried;

"Is there a creek or a pond outside somewhere? I thought I heard running water outside my window last night."

"Yes, just at the back of the house and down a little through the woods. You will have a pleasant time exploring around here," her grams said, as she brought her a plate of pancakes and a glass of orange juice. She sat down also after bringing herself a plate and coffee. Chloe eagerly attacked her pancakes, they were delicious. Just then Rowena rounded the door jam on the way to her water bowl. Chloe held her hand out to her.

"Here Rowena, come here kitty," she beckoned. Rowena turned her head and hissed nastily.

"I think that cat hates me."

"Don't worry… she is cranky to most everyone. Honestly, I don't even know why she's here. She just appeared seemingly from nowhere shortly after Grandpa Jack returned from India. She just somehow included herself into the household. At the time I was so overwhelmed with Jacks' return; I just let her in and went with it. I can't say I haven't more than once questioned myself about it. And yet … here she still is."

Chloe finished her breakfast and brought her plate and glass over to the sink.

"Go ahead and just leave those there; we can clean up at dinner time," Grandma Jen said, adding;

"Rowena may warm up to you yet, sometimes she surprises me. You may want to go out and explore the creek outside, it's very nice. I will put some cookies in a little bag for you to snack on while you're out there."

"Ok, that sounds nice, thank you. I'll go get my hat, as it's very sunny outside," Chloe said, as she excitedly ran out of the kitchen and bounded up the stairs.

When she got to her room, she went to look out the window. She noticed Rowena was out there walking towards the barn. She turned and went to her still unpacked suitcase next to her bed, and pulled out her favorite turquoise colored hat, which her father had given her just a short week ago… it saddened her to put it on.

She then turned and went back downstairs to the kitchen. Her grandma was just putting some cookies into a little brown paper bag for her. She folded the lip of it and handed it to her.

"Ok my angel, I'm sure you will have a pleasant time outside," she said, as she handed it to her.

"Yummy… thank you Grandma. Ok, I guess I'll go out now and play."

"Have fun, I'll be here straightening up the house and puttering around if you need me," Grandma Jen said, as she watched her exuberantly running from the kitchen and out the front door. It was a very warm and sunny morning. She was glad that she had put on her hat. She walked towards the barn, wondering if Rowena had gone in there.

Upon opening the door and entering, she noticed a few empty stalls where horses or other animals could be kept. It was somewhat dim inside, as the only other light source was coming from the other open door of the upper hay loft area. She went to a wooden ladder, which led up to it on her right, and climbed up.

Upon reaching the top, she made her way to the loft door and looked out. The view of the house and the forest beyond was beautiful and intriguing. She could also see parts of the creek peeking out at intervals between the trees. With her curiosity piquing, she made her way back down the ladder to go see it.

As she exited the barn, it was then that she noticed Rowena at the head of a little trail, just to the right side of the house. She was standing there with her head cocked back and looking at her... as if waiting for her to notice. Once their eyes met, Rowena then proceeded to disappear into the wooded trail.

"Ok, you've got my attention if that's what you wanted. I was headed in that direction any way," Chloe said, and then crossed the driveway and headed into the forest trail. It was lush with ferns and myriad blooming flowers, all fragrant and beautiful. She walked unhurriedly, pausing here and there to smell this one and that.

"I love this trail," she thought. Eventually, she came out some distance beyond the house. The creek was before her and running northerly to the right. As a creek goes, it was robust. It was too wide across, fast moving and deep to think of crossing it. It was then that she again noticed Rowena a short distance away, dawdling along downstream. She decided to follow her, and made her way along the creeks edge. It was easy going, as the trail continued along this path.

"My, this is just wonderful, I could come here every day and never tire of it," she thought. She walked slowly for some time, marveling at the new scenery of each twist and turn of the creek. She then came to a little perch at the top of a small hill. There was a tree with a small boulder at its base... perfect for sitting before upon the ground while resting ones' back while viewing the creek.

"Yes, this is a far enough walk for today," she said aloud, and sat down in the shade. She took off her hat and set it beside her.

"It's definitely time for some cookies," she said, as she reached into the bag a grabbed a sizable cookie, raised it to her mouth, and took a bite.

"Wow, grandma makes great cookies," she thought, as she quickly finished it and grabbed another one. As she took another bite and looked further along the trail, down the little hill from where she was, she noticed a kind of old suspension bridge that crossed the creek. She could see from here that it was in obvious disrepair, as quite a few of the wooden foot planks were hanging loose. The creek was also speeding up before that as it traversed more steeply downhill.

She thought; "Hmmm…that bridge looks fun to cross over… but if I try it, I'll have to go slow and be careful that it's safe."

It was then that she noticed some movement from back along the trail. About one hundred feet away, she could see a mouse walking along on its hind legs…and using…a walking stick? "Oh my god… not again!" she thought. Just then, she heard a rustling of bushes immediately behind her.

As she turned her head to look, Rowena was already springing to her side from them, and in one swoop she had Chloe's favorite hat in her mouth and was running past her down the path towards the bridge. Chloe uncontrolledly screamed out loud, and sprang to her feet in pursuit. Rowena ran across the bridge, effortlessly jumping over the missing and loose planks.

Chloe reached the bridge and momentarily slowed to assess the condition of it. She couldn't slow down and let Rowena get away with the hat her father had just recently given her! She tore along it headlong in hot pursuit. Rowena had already reached the other side and was disappearing into the forest.

Suddenly Chloe became frightened as she ran... the planks were creaking and snapping in half as she reached the middle of the bridge. Her adrenalin was flowing as she then stepped upon the one fatal plank which made a loud cracking noise. Time seemed to slow down as her brains' thoughts moved so quickly. She seemingly watched herself from a distance away as the plank broke, and she was falling through the bottom of the bridge, while screaming in terror. She hit and went under the frigid water with a thudding splash, then quickly got her head above water as she kicked her feet and flailed her arms about.

She was normally a good swimmer, but water had gotten up her nose, and somewhat into her lungs. She coughed and choked painfully while somehow staying afloat as she was dragged quickly downstream. The water was spilling roughly over rocks and boulders, and she was starting to get alarmingly knocked about. She was having a hard time swimming to the shore as she was tossed among the rocks... and her heavy saturated clothes were adding to the problem.

She felt her strength waning as she struggled for each breath and arm stroke, and if things seemed they couldn't get much worse than they already were, she noticed up ahead that the creek suddenly disappeared into a white spray of mist, accompanied by a deafening roar. Could there impossibly be a waterfall coming up? This was now a deadly, desperate situation, and she felt that she was starting to lose all hope.

Just then, she caught sight of the mouse on the bank ahead. And it was using its walking stick in trying to pry loose a small rock on the hill side, which was supporting a larger rock with a large dead tree branch lying atop of it. "Oh, please let that work....it's my only chance to survive this," she thought.

Then, its exertions were rewarded as the mouse fell forwards head over heels when the small rock dislodged. Sure enough, it started an avalanche of rocks, boulders, and the tree limb, which all spilled into the creek before her, with the large limb lodging diagonally into the creek floor. With a half a second to spare, she came upon it and grabbed a protruding branch.

She felt she had to move quickly, who knows how long it would all stay stationary. With her last remaining strength, she pulled her heavy self onto the limb and stood upon it. And no sooner did she stand, that it began to give way. She leaped off of it and onto the accompanying boulders, jumping from one to the other as they in turn dislodged. She made it to the bank, and couldn't believe it. As she lay there on her back to catch her breath, she was so exhausted she couldn't move, and before she knew it, fell into a deep recuperative slumber.

Chapter 3

Chloe awoke to the feeling of cold dampness. She opened her eyes and found she was lying someplace on the ground outside near a creek. The feeling of disorientation lasted only a few moments before everything came flooding back. She sat up. The mess of the avalanche, she remembered, now looked indiscernible in the tumultuous torrent. And it was now much later in the day. She wondered how long she had slept… maybe a few hours.

There was no sign of the mouse that had saved her life. And of course that miserable Rowena was nowhere to be seen. "That cat will be very sorry the next time I chance upon her," she thought. She attempted to stand up and failed the first time, all the muscles in her body were tight and still recuperating. She was successful the second time, albeit not painlessly, and began her slow and limping progress back to Grandma Jen's.

As she finally neared the house, she decided that she wouldn't tell grams anything of what had happened, it was all just too fantastical... probably not to be believed by anyone of sane mind. She would only say she fell into the creek if questioned about her wet clothes.

When she went in the front door, she peeked around the kitchen entrance...Grandma Jen was busy making their dinner. She backed up and forcibly pushed the front screen door wide open, allowing her time to bolt to the stairs undetected. It noisily slammed as she simultaneously yelled;

"Hi Grandma, I'm home... I'm going up to shower and change clothes!"

"Ok!" her grandma said. The hot shower and dry clothes washed away most of her morass. She came back down the stairs and entered the kitchen. Grandma Jen had just finished plating their dinner... delicious looking and smelling fried chicken, mashed potatoes and gravy, and corn on the cob. Chloe said;

"Oh My Gosh, I'm famished!" Grandma Jen looked at her and laughed heartily. "Ha ha...here you go... bon appetite," she said, as she handed her the plate. Chloe turned and placed it on the table. She went and poured herself a glass of milk and returned and sat at the table across from her grandma. Without so much as a word, she polished off the whole plate.

"My, you certainly were not kidding. I will get you another plate," her grandma said, as she rose to get her another. She placed another full dinner in front of her and then sat down to finish her own.

"I take it you enjoyed exploring outside today, you were gone quite a long time and I began to get a little worried," her grandma said.

"Yes I did very much, thank you." Her Grandma adoringly watched her finish her second helping.

"You know, it wasn't until after you left this morning that I thought to tell you to be careful if you happened upon the bridge that crosses the creek, it's quite old and very much in disrepair, did you see it?"

"Yes, I did...and you are right. It looked quite treacherous so I stayed clear of it," she lied.

"Oh good... I would never have forgiven myself if something happened to you there and I had forgotten to tell you of it."

"Yes I spent a lot of time at the creek, I followed Rowena there. It's very beautiful. Have you seen Rowena around here lately?"

"No, come to think of it, I haven't seen her all day, but I'm sure she'll be back for dinner soon, she never misses a meal." Chloe then said to her;

"Thank you very much for having me here Grandma, I like it very much."

"You're welcome Chloe, I'm glad. I've very much loved living here these many years." Chloe offered,

"Would you let me wash the dishes for us? I'd like to help out around here."

"Well aren't you sweet, sure...that would help." Chloe rose and took both their empty plates to the sink and began to clean them. Grandma Jen brought her cup and set it beside her on the counter, saying;

"If you don't mind I think I'll retire to my room and read for a while in bed. I may fall asleep in the process as usual, so please excuse me if you don't hear from me the rest of the evening. I'm going to lock the front door...don't worry about Rowena, she finds her own way in through her cat door at the rear of the house."

"Ok, I definitely won't worry about her. Good night Grandma."

"Goodnight," Grandma Jen replied, as she left the kitchen and went up the stairs. "I definitely won't worry about Rowena," Chloe thought. She finished cleaning up the kitchen. It was easy for her, as she had the same chore at home.

She suddenly felt sad again as she thought about her mommy and daddy… and her old home being a thing of the past. She cast her eyes dejectedly to the floor…and with her head bowed; she turned off the kitchen light and headed up the stairs to her room.

Once in her room, she went to the window and opened it. She nervously peeked out to look where she had before seen that creature. Thank god it was nowhere around there now. But somehow she felt that she probably would be seeing it again though, as this tree was most likely its home. Well, she wasn't going to worry about that right now. She felt tired after that huge meal.

She went down the hall to the bathroom and brushed her teeth. When she came back she decided she would leave the hall light on to alleviate her nervousness and turned off the light in her room. She hopped into bed and quickly fell asleep while hugging the teddy bear.

A few dreamless hours had lapsed when Chloe again opened her eyes. She was still hugging the teddy bear and hadn't moved an inch. She was lying on her side and her back was to the door. The hall light was still on and shedding light into the room.

She could see a full moon through the window above the large branch of the tree. Suddenly she noticed a large moving shadow was being cast upon the wall next to the window from the light of the hallway…it looked monstrously large and menacing, and she was startled with fright! She hugged the bear tighter and turned her head to steal a peek at what certainly must be some behemoth standing there, ready to pounce on and eat her. But when she looked, she was relieved but confused to see that nothing was there. Then some movement along floor caught her eye. It was her little mouse…and it was scurrying away. It headed towards the stairs and then bounded up them.

She felt very thankful to that mouse for saving her life, and also felt she needed to somehow say thank you to it. She got out of bed and went to the door while still holding the teddy bear. When she got there she noticed Rowena was just coming up the stairs from below. She felt a jolt of anger upon seeing that cat, as she was sure Rowena had purposefully tried to do her in earlier.

She forcefully lobbed the teddy bear at her. Rowena tried to dodge the attack, but was pegged right in the face. With a shriek, she tumbled backwards and noisily clattered all the way to the bottom of the stairs along with the teddy bear. "I got you, you miserable wretch!" Chloe said, as she rushed over there to look down. She saw the bear lying at the foot of the stairs, but Rowena was already gone…hopefully to nurse her wounds, she thought. "Good riddance!" Chloe said aloud.

She then looked up at the attic door on the third floor and noticed that it was slightly ajar. She quietly crept up the stairs to it and hovered there pensively, putting her hand upon the brass door knob, and her ear to the blackness...and froze with fright when she heard muffled voices coming from inside! How could there be voices in there; had someone maybe left a radio on? She tried to make out what was being said, and heard in succession;

"Maybe this is a good thing... she may be able to help."

"I don't see how, she is such a small thing."

"The tasks are too monumental... I'm beginning to lose all hope." And lastly, "We need to do something very soon or all is lost." Chloe was certain now that it was no radio she heard. With her heart hammering in her chest, she slowly pushed open the door. It made a loud and dry creaking sound. And when she stopped pushing it, she heard many muffled gasps...and the sounds of furniture being pushed upon a wooden floor...then all was quiet. In shock, she waited a few moments, but now heard nothing more than eerie silence.

With her curiosity piquing, she could stand it no longer and slipped into the darkness... then waited blindly for her eyes to adjust. Slowly she began see that there was a wall just before her... It must be the back of the room. She turned around and could see that the room was mostly to the left of the door and around a corner, which expanded towards the front of the house. She stepped around it, passing piles of bric-a-brac and what she guessed were pieces of furniture covered in white sheets, and came into the main part of the room, which was illuminated by the light of a full moon through some open French doors.

There she saw, among other things, were more pieces of furniture… but uncovered; a grandfather clock, a chest of drawers, an old vacuum cleaner, and a burgundy colored wing-back chair with another wooden chair just beside it. There were more shapes, but she couldn't make them out in the shadowy corners of the room. And there, in the middle of it all and spread out upon the floor, was an interesting antique Persian carpet… and just beyond that, the French doors of the small balcony, which were pushed open to the night.

A full moon was fully visible beyond the black silhouette of a tree branch and its' leaves. There was also another silhouette there as well… and there was no mistaking what it was.

It was that opossum hanging upside down from the branch, and she could see that its glinting eyes were looking at her. "Ok," she thought. "I'm tired of feeling frightened of this whole situation; it's time to face this all head on." With that, she strode bravely into the room and onto the center of the carpet, stopped, and put her hands upon her hips. Without saying anything, she stuck out her chin and waited for whatever may come. But only more silence answered her thoughts. "Well, is there anyone here? I heard someone talking about me…" she said.

"That you did little one, and we apologize for talking about you." Clearly it was the creature hanging from the branch which was again speaking to her. She kept her composure and resolve while standing there and looking at it. It did seem friendly enough… and amusingly, it again had that distinctively perfect British accent. She couldn't help but giggle, then replied;

"Hello Mr. Opossum, we've almost spoken before. Please forgive me for being startled the last time. You see, I'm not used to strange animals…or any animals for that matter… speaking to me." He then acknowledged;

"Yes, this is all a highly unusual circumstance at this house I'm afraid. My friends have taken to calling me Mr. Oppum... and what may I ask is your name little one?"

"I'm Chloe; it's nice to make your acquaintance Mr. Oppum."

"Likewise," he replied.

"Excuse me... I did hear you say 'we'...but I don't see anyone else here." Just then, her little mouse popped its head out from around the base of an old piano, which was in the shadows, against the wall and to the right of the French doors.

"Hello, it's nice to finally meet you Chloe," it said, as it walked into view before her. Chloe again found the situation amusing and ludicrous. Giggling more uncontrollably this time, she answered;

"Well hello again my little friend, I've so wanted to thank you for helping me earlier today...thank you Mr. ..."

"My friends have taken to calling me Monty, and you're welcome."

"Yes it is nice to finally meet you as well Monty. Are there any more talking animals around here that I may want to meet?" Monty looked up at Mr. Oppum, then looked back to her and said;

"Well, as far as animals go, there is only one more that we know of that speaks, and it's that miserable Rowena."

"Yes, I know that miserable Rowena. And I'm also sure that she means me harm. I had an almost fateful run in with her today...Monty could attest to that."

"Yes, you most certainly did, but I'm happy to see that you're now safe and sound."

"Excuse me Monty, but you said 'as far as animals go' about speaking...I'm a little confused." Monty again looked to Mr. Oppum, they shared a knowing stare for a few moments, then he looked back to Chloe and said;

"Well, we have more friends that would be happy to meet you…" Chloe replied;

"Really, I would so much like to make more friends here; who are they?" Just then, there was simultaneous movement and commotion around the room which certainly caught her off guard. The pianos' keys erupted in musical notes, accompanied with speech; the chest of drawers legs moved along with speech coming out of its' sliding drawers; the vacuum cleaner erupted into a whirring motor sound of speech, with its' front light coming on and its' dangling cord dancing around; the corners of the rug where she stood fluttered; and the wing-back and wooden chairs' legs moved to curtsy, as chorus of greetings, all a jumble, reached her ears and shocked her brain!

"Hello Chloe, it's so nice to meet you!" Uncontrolledly, she jumped with a start and staggered backwards a few steps, falling harmlessly but noisily onto a pile of rubble, which stirred up a small cloud of dust and cob webs.

When the dust cleared, she lay there a few moments looking upon this impossible scene. They were now all quiet again, but she thought she could still discern all of those previously speaking and moving objects, ever so slightly leaning in her direction, as if poised and waiting for her to speak.

She slightly shivered with fright. Then, in a little quivering voice, she managed;

"Hello…it's nice to meet you all." The wing-back chairs' arms then moved as its' front legs also bowed towards her a little, and she heard a matronly voice reply;

"I'm so sorry if we all startled you dear, but please believe me when I tell you that we are also frightened to speak to you as well. We have never spoken to a human before, and we're afraid of the possible consequences of doing so." Chloe replied to her;

"You would be afraid of a little girl like me?"

"Yes, if humans learned of our secret… we don't know what would become of us. We would probably be taken from this place to who knows where." Chloe pulled herself from the rubble, and while brushing off the dust, she said;

"Oh, please don't worry. I'm good at keeping secrets, and I promise I won't tell a soul!" A sigh of relief was heard around the room.

There was then a quiet little chime of piano, with an accompanying, friendly sounding male voice;

"That is a tremendous relief to all of us to hear you say that, thank you little Chloe."

"Oh please, don't mention it. I feel so lucky and honored to have such wonderful new friends," she said, and looked around the room at all of them; Mr. Oppum, Monty, wing-back chair, wooden chair, chest of drawers, piano, vacuum cleaner, and the Persian carpet… and continued;

"Excuse me, maybe it's none of my business, but how on earth did this all come to be? I'm feeling the most insatiable curiosity about it, and I'm ready to literally explode!"

Mr. Oppum swung himself to a sitting position atop his branch and began:

"Well you see… it is the most fantastical story really, perhaps it's Mr. Carpets' place to begin this tale." They all looked at the carpet. Then one of its corners' fluttered;

"Well, I'm too happy to comply. You see, I'm not originally from this house, my home was in India. I was once an ordinary lifeless rug. Then, one day I awoke and noticed I was in a great room of gilded furniture, hanging tapestries, and golden vases. I could also hear what I later learned was music. And I saw that many people were standing upon me and all around an expansive room."

"The one person that I could not help but especially notice was standing on the center of me. He had a turban of midnight blue upon his head which was ornamented with a large intense looking jewel. As soon as I looked upon that jewel a feeling of hot fire momentarily engulfed my being. It was impossible for me to deny the condition of my new found consciousness was emanating from that enchanting stone."

"From that point on I was awake. I watched the comings and goings of many people, heard the conversations of daily life, and was a witness to all that transpired there. I had no concept of time initially, so how much of it passed I do not know. But there was much joy that I could feel there in the family of the palace, and of the many guests that frequented there."

"But after a time as I lay there, the mood of the palace began to darken and the great parties dwindled in frequency. This room also doubled as a state room, and off to one end of it was a dais upon which was a large golden throne. In the past, all manner of business was conducted there between the subjects of the kingdom and the bejeweled one who sat upon the throne. They called him your Majesty, or Maharaja Rajeem. I witnessed many friendly and fair judgments that most always ended in contentment. But increasingly towards the end of my days there, the affairs of the room became a continuous stream of dread. People always left crying and had to be dragged out. The subject matter of the conversations at that time were still too challenging for me to understand."

"I understood my consciousness was created by Rajeems' jewel and I considered that a wonderful miracle. There were other miracles happening there as well. There was a haram there of many beautiful women, and they had a small pet monkey that wore a little red hat with a hanging tassel and was clothed in a green velvet vest and short red pants."

"It freely wandered the palace, and often sat upon myself while eating fruit from the bowl on the great table. I had heard it being called Moki. After being familiar with him for some time, one night he was again sitting upon me eating a guava. He was making all manner of undignified noises, as this was a troublesomely over ripened piece of fruit."

"Then, as he bit into it yet again, it squirted a mess of juice all over his clothing. And as it did he uncontrolledly blurted out speech and said;"

"Oh bother!"

"He then alarmingly clapped his hand over his mouth and looked around the room. I supposed it was to see if there was anyone around that had noticed him speak. Immediately he looked relieved, as no one was there. I was sure that monkeys should not have the power to speak as humans do, and I wondered if we both shared the same enchantment."

"Then I wondered for the first time if I could also speak, so I mustered up the courage to try and said,"

"Ah…hello?" "I noticed a small corner of me flapped as well. Moki dropped his fruit and stood alarmingly. He stared at me beneath his feet for a few moments, and then walked my perimeter, lifting each corner as he passed. Finally he sat down, and as he continued to stare at me he said;"

"Hello…did you say something?" "I answered;
Yes I did…I'm just now finding that I can speak. Can you understand me? Moki's jaw then dropped."

"Yes I can. I've heard of magic carpets before, and that they can fly! ...are you a magic carpet?"

"I thought for a moment about this and answered; I'm sorry; I don't understand the meaning of the word fly."

"It means that you can float on the air above the ground."

"Well...honestly I don't know."

"My name is Moki, it's nice to meet you Mr. Magic carpet." "Thank you, it's nice to make your acquaintance Mr. Moki. Actually, I've known your name for quite some time, as I've been lying here and observing things for some time now." Moki countered;

"This is truly astonishing. I've so wanted to meet another magical friend. I consider myself so because I've yet to hear another animal or inanimate object speak until now...will you be my friend?" "But of course! I said."

"I'm so happy... my own secret friend! But you must be very careful, we're not supposed to be able to speak, if we're ever heard speaking, I'm not sure how the humans would react and what would become of us!"

"Thank you for alerting me, I shall be very careful."

"I'm still very curious though if you are able to float upon the air." "Well If I am a magic carpet as you say...maybe I can, shall I try?"

"Oh yes, please try!"

"The thought of even moving for me was so foreign, and flying was even more so. But to my amazement as soon as I tried, I began to effortlessly rise above the ground. I couldn't believe it...there I was with Moki still perched upon myself, and both of us floating above the ground! Moki then exclaimed,"

"Oh what a wonderful day my new friend Mr. Magic carpet!" "As he excitedly jumped up and down upon me, we must have been quite a sight. Moki then said,"

"Oh, but quickly, quickly you must lower us back to the floor lest we be seen!" "I then lowered us back to the floor."

"Moki and I sat and conversed most quietly all through that night as he gobbled up all the fruit. He told me that he also felt his gifts were the result of that miraculous jewel in the Maharaja Rajeem's turban. He also relayed to me all the gossips of the palace and the current dark circumstances surrounding the place. He said that Rajeem initially used his power for the good of the people of the palace and his kingdom. But he had noticed for some time now that everything had changed for the worse."

"One of the frequent visitors, an American government official, recently came to visit Rajeem to voice concerns that he felt Rajeem was exerting too much control over the rest of the world. He said he didn't know how, but all the rulers of the world were suddenly obeying all of his commands."

"At that point Rajeem had his guards grab him. They beat him and dragged him down to a dungeon beneath the palace and imprisoned him. Then, one quiet night when everyone in the palace was asleep, Moki said that he decided to seek out the prisoner to see what had become of him."

"He crept stealthily down the cold narrow stone steps to where he imagined he would find him. At the end of a long corridor lit by a lone torch on the wall, he saw a sleeping guard upon a chair before a heavy wooden door. There were bars on the door above the guards' head, so he quietly hopped up and slipped through them and into the cell."

"In a corner he found the man sleeping on a cot, and after awakening and surprising him of a speaking monkey, Moki told him that he wanted to help him escape. The American told him his name was Jack. After much discussion, it became apparent to them that Rajeem's power resided in the eerie jewel of his turban."

"They then devised a plan to steal it from Rajeem and Jack would escape with it. Moki then went immediately to Rajeems sleeping quarters, filched the stone from his turban on the dressing table as he slept, and then returned to the stone corridor. He carefully unclasped the cell keys from the guards' belt and unlocked the door. Jack then surprised the sleeping guard and bound and gagged him."

"Their plan involved me to fly the American out from the open balcony and far away from the palace. Moki had told me of their plans previously and I agreed to help. Everything went without a hitch, and the last I saw of Moki was when Jack and I were quietly floating away into the night. We called out our farewells to him and began our journey to this house."

Mr. Oppum cleared his throat to gain their attention.

"Now you see Chloe, all of us here were affected in the same manner once the stone was brought here."

"Yes…I understand. Then you all must know that Jack was my Grandpa. So where is this magic jewel…is it still here?" The piano sadly chimed;

"No, it is most definitely not. At first it was hidden by your Grandpa jack in this very room…inside our friend here." The bureaus top drawer slid open and it continued;

"Yes, right here inside of me. And that is where it stayed until that miserable Rowena started poking around up here and tricked me into opening my drawer... no sooner than I did is when a crow swooped in through these open doors here, and snatched it right up and flew away with it!" Monty added;

"Yes, we're now sure that Rowena was somehow sent here by Rajeem for that very purpose."

Chloe scratched her head, and queried;

"I'm not sure, but before I came in here, did I hear you all talking about me somehow helping you with something?" Mr. Oppum answered;

"Well you see...we have for a while now been in a state of alarm and grief." He pointed to the grandfather clock off to the side of them. "He was our good friend Mr. Grandfather Clock... always merrily chiming away the quarter hours and keeping us in jolly good company. Then one day, not too long ago, he just ceased to be. I mean, he is still there as a clock...but he no longer talks to us...he is...dead." Tears welled up in Mr. Oppums eyes. There was then a deafening silence in the room.

Chloe could see that they were all very sad to lose their friend. The vacuum whirred;

"Yes, we are very sad that we no longer have our friend the clock. And we are also, of course, horrified that at any moment any of us could also cease to be alive as well!" Chloe was shocked, and then lamented;

"Oh my, that is truly frightening. But what could I possibly do to help you all?" Monty countered;

"Well, we're not sure. We need to make a plan to get the stone back here, and out of the hands of that evil man...nothing good can come from him having possession of it."

Chloe thought about this for a moment.

"My goodness, it seems that we may be the only ones aware of this pending calamity!" Monty replied;

"So then you do see… we must do something. Mr. Oppum and I have already planned to ride Mr. Magic Carpet there to do this…but it is such a monumental task." Mr. Oppum added;

"Yes, and also we have thought that we could ultimately fail if we ceased to be aware, like Mr. Clock here, before we were successful in regaining the stone." Chloe raised both her fists above her head.

"Then I will go with you three, and we shall be determined to save ourselves and the whole world!" They all danced and hooted in shared enthusiasm. Wing back chair then said;

"Oh, thank you Chloe for agreeing to help us!" Chloe answered;

"You are most welcome. So we must begin our plans for this journey." Magic carpet flapped;

"From what I remember, it took several days of flight from India to this house. And your Grandpa Jack said it was very cold, and sometimes it rained." Chloe said;

"Then we better bring warm blankets… and a small tent that we can erect upon Mr. Carpet." Monty suddenly exclaimed;

"We are in luck, there is just such a tent right in this room!" He proceeded to scamper off into the shadows and dove into a pile of junk.

They all watched as bric-a-brac and whatnots were thrown hither and thither, then his little head popped up from an adjoining pile and quipped;

"I've found it… I knew it was here somewhere, but I need help pulling it out!" Chloe ran over to help. Mr. Oppum swung off his perch by his tail, and also ran over to help as everyone else turned to watch. The three of them simultaneously began pulling on a corner of the tent fabric. With their heels dug in and the sounds of straining grunts, it finally came free with a billowing of tent material, and the spectacle of heads over heels. They came to rest back at the center of Mr. Carpet, all a tangle of arms, legs, and heads, protruding from the mess of twisted fabric.

All of the room laughed and joked with one another as the three untangled themselves while piano played a comedic tune. Once done, Monty said;

"Well, that's done. I shall now get back to work finding the other missing bits of the tent." And he scampered back and dove again into the pile. Chloe and Mr. Oppum also began rummaging through it to look for the pieces, as well as the blankets they needed, and anything else that looked like a necessity.

During all the commotion of the last hour, no one had noticed that their efforts and conversations had not gone unnoticed by another occupant of the house. In the dark, back by the door of the attic, if one looked carefully… two green eyes peered at them. Rowena muttered to herself under her purring breath;

"Purr… so they are all so smug in thinking I will allow them their plans." She then backed further into the shadows to watch, undetected, while devising her own sinister counter plans.

Chapter 4

After they had left a pile of the necessary items found for their journey at the center of Mr. Carpet, Chloe was feeling sleepy and wished them all a good night. Back in her room and sitting cross legged upon her bed in the dark, she looked out the window at the full moon between the tree branches and thought;

"Wow, what a truly incredible evening it has been." A single large shiver shook her whole body as she realized the magnitude of the nights' events. Then a feeling of doubt crept into her mind. How could she go on such an important, dangerous, and fantastical journey? And how could she just disappear from Grandma Jen and the rest of her family without making them sick with worry?

She suddenly felt exhausted, as it was all so much of an overload for her poor little head. She got under the covers and immediately fell asleep.

When she awoke the next morning, she immediately sat again into her cross legged position. She noticed the sun was already in a midmorning position. Suddenly, she was astonished that during her lengthy slumber, her busy, dreamless mind had already somehow hatched a workable plan on how to make the journey without alarming her family.

She would write a letter addressed to herself that was made to look as if it came from her Auntie Meg. In it would be a round trip bus ticket that she would purchase herself. The letter would state that Chloe was needed to be present for a reading of the will of her parents, along other poignant matters.

"Well," she thought, "Good work girl, now I will just have to wait for Grandma Jen to take me into town on her next grocery shopping trip." Hopefully, she also thought, that while Grams shopped, she would be able to slip away long enough to run over to the bus station and purchase the ticket. She had noticed that on the way to this house the first day here, that the town was not too far away, and she would be able to walk back here undetected after supposedly leaving town on the bus. Then she would wait until the evening when Grams was asleep from reading in bed, and have Mr. Oppum or Monty unlock the front door for her. "Hmmm…," she thought, "everything hinges upon the bus station being close enough to the grocery store for me to have time to dash over there without Grams noticing that I'm gone."

"And also secondly, that Grandma Jen does not call Auntie Meg to confirm my trip. I will have to time the arrival of the letter with my departure date being very soon… like maybe the very next morning so there is less time for telephone calls to be made."

Feeling satisfied with her plan, Chloe excitedly sprang from her bed, hurriedly dressed for the day, and clambered downstairs to see if Grams was in the kitchen where she usually was at this time of the morning. Once she got there, she noticed that of course she was. Chloe sat at the table by the window and began to steer the conversation towards her plan.

"Good morning Grandma."

"Good morning Chloe, you slept late this morning...that's good."

"Yes I did...um, we haven't gone into town yet... do you need to go grocery shopping soon?"

"As a matter of fact, since you mention it...the fridge' is getting a little bare. Maybe today would be a good time to go, would you like to go?"

"Sure, that sounds good."

"All right then, after you have your breakfast I will go upstairs and get ready to go." Chloe thought, "Well, that couldn't have been any easier." Chloe had her late breakfast, coupled with a lovely chat. She really loved the mornings with her Grandma. After the dishes were done they both went upstairs to get ready. In her room, Chloe found her little stash of money and put it into her pocket, then went down stairs and out into the front yard by her Grandmas' car to wait for her.

Before long they were motoring towards town. Chloe kept her eyes peeled for a bus station once they entered the town, and sure enough... there was the Greyhound Bus station as plain as day. It really was quite a small town she noticed, and it would be no problem to run from one end of it to the other in the space of just a few minutes. Well that was a relief. Once they were inside the store and puttering down the aisles with the shopping basket Chloe excused herself to go find the restroom.

Once she got to the end of the aisle, she looked back and saw Grams was busy reading the fine print of some jar of something. "Now's the time… it's all or nothing," she thought, and calmly walked nonchalantly to the front door. With one last look back to make sure no one was watching her, which there wasn't; she turned and ran as fast as she could to the station.

Luckily, it was fairly empty of patrons there at the moment and there was no one waiting in line at the ticket counter. She had with her the self-addressed envelope, and she had also given much thought about the timing of the mailing of it. If there was a bus leaving to her home town three days from now, it could just possibly work perfectly… given it would only take one day for the local post office to deliver the letter back to her Grandmas house.

Once at the counter, she pressed her freckled nose above the counter and saw the attendant busy rubber stamping the days tickets. He had a friendly chubby looking face with round wire rimmed glasses which were too small for his face. He stopped what he was doing when he noticed her and asked;

"Well, good morning little Miss, may I help you with something?"

"Yes please, my Grandma asked me to come over here while she was shopping to purchase a ticket to Los Angeles for myself. She said it would be a nice chore for me to do, to help her save time this morning, as we're very busy today. Do you have a bus that leaves for that destination in three days from today?"

"Why yes we do… a bus travels from here to there every day. Would you like to buy a ticket?"

"Yes please… round trip." He stamped her ticket with his rubber stamp and pushed it over to her. She paid the money he requested and asked;

"Do you happen to have a postage stamp that I could buy?"

"I certainly do…its thirty five cents." She also bought the stamp, turned and went to some chairs by the wall and sat for a moment while licking and affixing the stamp. After sealing the envelope with the letter and ticket placed inside, she ran back outside towards the grocery store. The post office was on the same street and it was just a matter of tossing the letter into the mail box in front of it as she bolted by.

When she got back to the store, she stopped and peeked into the door to see if Grams was anywhere to be seen. There she was just getting to the back of a short line at the checkout counter. Chloe walked to the other door at the opposite end of the store, went in and took the long way around to the back of the store, then walked to the front and joined her grandma at the checkout.

"Oh, there you are. I was beginning to worry about where you were."

"Sorry, I had a little tummy ache and sat on a bench, but it's gone now."

"Well, I'm glad you're feeling better now. It looks like we're finished with our shopping for the day. I don't have any other errands today, so I guess we'll go straight home… oh, by the way, I bought you two kinds of ice cream. You weren't around so I chose chocolate and burgundy cherry. Do you like those flavors?"

"Oh yes! Thank you Grandma!"

"You're quite welcome." During their short trip home, Chloe thought how relieved she was that so far her plan seemed to be working. Once they were home and the groceries were put away, she helped herself to a large bowl of delicious ice cream. With the bowl in her hands and the spoon stuck vertically into it, she made like she was going up to her room to enjoy it.

When she got to her bedroom door she closed it a little noisily to make it sound as if she went inside... then turned and quietly crept up the stairs to the attic. She squished herself through the partly opened door, not wanting to move it lest it squeak like it usually did, and then proceeded to sit at the center of Mr. Carpet.

"Hello Mr. Carpet, and every one, how are you all doing today?" For a few moments there was no answer and she was horrified that either she had imagined the whole thing, or worse yet they were all gone. Then all at once they all answered in a jumble of hellos. "Good morning Chloe," "Hello," "Hi Chloe," and, "Nice to see you again Chloe."

She took a bite of her ice cream and noticed Mr. Oppum was sleeping upside down behind some leaves upon his branch. She remembered opossums prefer to sleep during the day time. Just then, Monty emerged from behind Piano, wiping the sleep from his eyes. Chloe said;

"Well, good morning Mr. sleepy head, you will be proud of me today. I went to town this morning and set in motion the plan of my secret departure for our journey." Monty sat in front of her mirroring her crossed legs. He seemed most interested in what she was eating.

"Good morning Chloe. Say, what is that?"

"It's chocolate and burgundy cherry ice cream, would you like to try some?"

"Oh, yes please." She lowered a spoonful to his little mouth and he nibbled a taste.

"My goodness, that is delectable. Might I have some as well?" Chloe replied;

"I have quite a bit of it here; I will share it with you." She looked around her immediate area and spied an old magazine lying nearby. She grabbed and plopped it between them on the floor and spooned a generous portion onto it. Just before he began eating it, he asked;

"So, what is your plan?"

"I've mailed myself a letter that's disguised to be from my Auntie. It also has in it a bus ticket for me which gives me an excuse to leave here. It should arrive tomorrow or the next day. When it does arrive, we shall need to leave the following evening. But I would first have to secretly make my way back into the house undetected after I fake my departure, so I will need you to unlock the door for me."

"Ok, I don't see a problem there. It looks like we have some more work to do today in getting our tent erected and secured, as well as gathering together all the other things we will need."

"Yes, you are quite right," Chloe replied. They took their time finishing their ice cream while discussing what other items they may need, which included; blankets, pillows, food, water, a flashlight, matches, warm clothes, a long rope, any money she might have, a pair of scissors or a knife in case they needed to cut something, and last but not least her tooth brush. Towards the end of their conversation Chloe noticed that it was well past noon now, and that they needed to start focusing on the tent.

Just then she heard Mr. Oppum rustling around in the leaves of his perch, and then saw him swing himself into a sitting position upon his branch. He said;

"Good afternoon everyone, I hope I wasn't snoring," as he stretched his arms over his head and yawned.

"Not this time… thank goodness," Vacuum Cleaner whirred. Piano then chimed;

"I shall play us some music while we're busy with our chores." And as he proceeded to play a rag, the three of them assembled the tent and secured it to Mr. Carpet.

"That feels quite secure, I think it will hold there just fine," said Mr. Carpet. Chloe then offered;

"Yes, I think we have done an adequate job. Now we need to find a small chest to store all of our other items in… I think I see one over there," she pointed off towards a dark corner. Mr. Oppum scampered over to it and then pulled it over to them, commenting, "Yes it does seem to fit the bill perfectly."

They then secured it as well at the rear, just behind the tent. Chloe then opened the lid and they started packing the blankets, pillows, and some canned food with an opener, paper plates and utensils that she found in a cupboard in the kitchen. They were industrious, and lucky enough to have found all the other afore mentioned items on their list as well. Chloe stated;

"We've made very good progress today; it really looks as if we are packed and ready to go. Now all we have to do is wait and hope everything else goes as planned." The chest of drawers' top drawer opened a little and said;

"Oh, thank heavens… it is really beginning to look like we do indeed have a prayer of saving ourselves. Thank you so much Chloe for coming to our aid." They all agreed and many thanks were heard from around the room.

"You're all quite welcome, thank you all as well for believing in me to be up to the task. I think I better not spend any more time up here today; I don't want my grandma to come looking for me and find us engaged up here. I will leave you now and check in tomorrow to let you know if the letter arrived, bye all…" she said and waved good bye as she slipped through the door. She heard their good byes as she tip toed down the stairs.

Chloe decided to get some fresh air, so she went on a walk towards the gorge. While walking on the path she decided to stop and relax at the same spot where Rowena had stolen her hat. She sat on the ground and put her back to the tree and rested her eyes. The sound of the water was relaxing, but a little disquieting from the memory of its chilling depths.

After a time she felt totally relaxed as the bright sun bleached its' warmth on her closed eyelids. While listening to the lulling foam, she began to hear another sound dispersed along with it coming from somewhere very near... was it... purring? Then there came an unfamiliar and not all together friendly sounding female voice;

"Purr... you and your stupid friends will fail you know... purr." Chloe opened her eyes and jumped up with a start. Grabbing a nearby dead branch to use as a club, she whirled around to see who it was. She saw Rowena's little head protruding from a bush close to where she had been sitting, and retorted;

"My friends are not stupid, and we will not fail. And also, if I have anything to do with it, you will get what you deserve!"

"Purr... what I deserve? I deserve praise. And before long I will again be by my master's side, serving and protecting him... purr."

"Not if I can help it!" She raised the club and swung it right at that smug little face, just missing it as it disappeared. She heard Rowena darting away through the brush, so she ran back along the path towards the house in chase.

When she got there she checked the perimeter of the house and nearby areas. The miserable thing was nowhere to be seen. She then noticed it was getting to be dusk now and it was time to be getting back inside, as she could also smell dinner cooking. She was about to throw her club back into the forest, but stopped mid stance. No, she would keep it for protection from now on. As she went through the front door and stopped at the kitchen entrance, she held the club behind herself.

"Hello Chloe, dinners' ready," Grandma Jen said as she eyed her suspiciously. Chloe answered her with a mischievous smile,

"Ok, I'll go wash up." She backed away and ran upstairs.

Dinner was comprised of corned beef, cabbage, and pleasant chit chat... and when all was finished and Chloe was once again cross legged upon her bed after brushing her teeth, she was greeted by Mr. Oppum as he sat on his usual perch just beyond the open window.

"Good evening Chloe," he said to her.

"Good evening Mr. Oppum, I'm feeling a little nervous about our upcoming trip."

"Yes, I am as well."

"I spoke to Rowena today for the first time... I think we need to be careful of her. She may be planning on sabotaging our plans..."

"Yes, we will definitely need to keep an eye out for her."

"I think it is time for me to be going to sleep now. My letter should be arriving with tomorrows' post and I must be a rested and convincing actress for my grandmother, so good night for now Mr. Oppum."

"Good night, I will be awake all night here and I will keep watch." Chloe pulled the covers over her head and was shortly fast asleep.

Chapter 5

The next morning was the usual breakfast with Grandma Jen followed by the kitchen tidying. Chloe felt nervous and fidgety all the while. The rest of the morning dragged along very slowly as she waited for the mail delivery. Then, finally she heard the familiar sound of the small mail delivery car buzzing up the drive way. She went out onto the front porch and sat on the bench. Grandma Jen came out shortly as she always did to retrieve it once it was placed in the box attached to one of the posts of the front steps.

"Thank you," grandma said while waving, and pulled out the small clump of mail. Leafing through it right there as usual, Chloe's heart skipped a beat as she spied her letter. Grandma Jen looked at it and said,

"Oh... here is one addressed to you...from your Auntie Meg!" And she handed it to her. Chloe took it and opened it, pulled out the letter and pretended to read it.

"Oh, there is a bus ticket in it as well," she said, as she fished it out of the envelope.

"It's a round trip ticket leaving tomorrow morning." She pretended surprise and handed it all to her Grams. Grandma Jen read through it.

"Well, it seems very important that we be sure to get you on that bus tomorrow morning, I guess you will be taking a little trip. I'm sorry... I hope the subject matter of this doesn't make you too sad today," she said, as she came over and gave Chloe a heartfelt hug. "Thank you...I'm feeling ok."

"Well, here you are. Best you go put in a safe place."

"All right," Chloe answered as she took it and went into the house to go put it away.

"My goodness," she thought, as she placed the letter onto her dressing table. "It's really happening!" She proceeded to pack a suitcase for her supposed bus trip. Well, she really was taking a trip; she may as well pack her clothes for her actual trip to India. After an hour or more, with her packing finished, she felt very antsy and did not quite know what to do next. She thought she better go find Monty and Mr. oppum to tell them the news. After cautiously craning her neck out of her bedroom door to see if the coast was clear, she crept up the stairs and slipped silently through the partially opened door.

Once at the center of Mr. Carpet, she looked around to see if they were anywhere about.

"Hello everyone, I've come to tell you that my plan to leave soon is in fact going to happen tomorrow night!"

"Oh, that is wonderful!" Said Mr. Carpet, followed by cheers from around the room. Monty then appeared from his usual spot from behind Mr. Piano, saying;

"Hello, that is good news. We must wake Mr. Oppum," he said as he walked to the open French doors, looked upwards and called out;

"Mr. Oppum… will you please wake up?" A small snoring snort was heard, along with the rustling of some leaves.

"Umm…umm…yes, I'm here…give me a moment." He swung upright upon his branch, continuing;

"Hello you two, what may I help you with?"

"Chloe says that the plan is to leave just tomorrow night!"

"Oh my…that is good news, thank you for waking me. Well…we are packed and ready to go, all we have to do is wait." Chloe added; "Yes, I'm also all packed and ready to go as well. Tomorrow morning my Grandma will take me to the bus station. I will try to get her to leave before the bus departs so I can avoid boarding it."

"I will then have to find a secluded place alongside the road someplace while on my way back here, to hide and wait the whole day away. And in the evening after my grandma has fallen asleep, Monty will unlock the front door for me so that I can get back in." "What a perfectly satisfying and mischievous plan… good show," retorted Mr. Oppum.

Monty then scurried off into the shadows, back towards the junk pile and said;

"I wanted to show you what else I found that I think we may have a need for, but I need help pulling it out." Chloe went over and grasped a brass handle that he was tugging on and lifted it before them.

"Why, it's a beautiful brass lantern. And also here is some fuel for it," she said, and pulled it as well from the pile and lifted it in her other hand, adding;

"Let us see if it works." They brought it back over to Mr. Carpet and sat down with it between them. While Chloe poured in the fuel, Monty said;

"I'll fetch the matches," and he hopped over and into their open storage chest. After some funny sounding little rummaging noises...his head popped up,

"Here they are," and hopped back over and handed them over. Chloe opened the small brass framed window, struck a match and lit the wick. A pleasant mellow glow emanated from it.

"You were right...this is perfect for lighting our way. Ok, I will extinguish it now." She blew it out and then secured it to the front of Mr. Carpet next to the rope that they had fastened there, which was to be their hand hold for securing themselves. Mr. Oppum then said; "I think some celebrating is in order, as we should reward ourselves for a job well done!" With that said, there was some happy singing, dancing, and merry making for not a short period of time.

As had happened before, there was a pair of unnoticed green eyes watching them with scrutiny from the shadows. Nothing was left unnoticed by Rowena as she surveyed the scene and formulated her plans for the following evening.

When the celebration came to an end, Chloe wished all of them a good night's sleep... excepting Mr. Oppum of course, and went down stairs to help Grandma Jen with their dinner. While eating their spaghetti and meatballs, Grandma Jen said;

"My, it sounded as if you were having a good time up there in the attic...you must have found my old Victrola buried up there amongst all that junk."

"Umm... yes I did grandma, I hope you don't mind."

"Oh, of course not, as long as you're enjoying yourself I'm happy." She continued;

"I noticed you are already packed for your trip tomorrow."

"Yes, I am all packed and ready to go. The ticket says the bus leaves at ten a.m., could you please bring and drop me off a little early…say around nine a.m.? I want to do a little personal shopping by myself to buy a gift for auntie and uncle."

"Sure, I don't see why not. But we must first see the station attendant to check if I need to sign any release for you to travel alone and have the driver watch over you." Chloe felt a little pang of worry, she hadn't thought of that. "I hope that nothing goes wrong," she thought.

After dinner, and with all the chores finished, Chloe excused herself to go to bed early. She then took a very long hot shower, as she thought this may be the last one in quite a while. Then she curled up in bed for a thorough night's sleep.

In the morning she arose, dressed herself, finalized packing her suitcase, and brought it down stairs. After setting it in the foyer near the front door, she joined her grandma in the kitchen for their breakfast. They talked about many things, her parents, her Grandpa Jack, and other family matters.

When they were finished eating, Chloe said;

"I guess I don't know exactly how long I will be away… I suppose it won't be for too long. My ticket is open on the return date. I suppose Auntie Meg and I will be calling to let you know when to be expecting me back."

"All right; I'm looking forward to your safe return, hopefully it isn't too long." They left the dishes unwashed in the sink, as it was time to get going. They went outside and loaded the suitcase into the trunk, got into the car and drove along the driveway towards the road. Along the way to town, Chloe kept her eyes open for a place that was suitable to hide for the day while waiting. After a couple of minutes she did see such a possible place…a kind of shady area near a little pond with some ducks floating around in it behind some trees.

When they got to town, grams parked the car at the bus station. Chloe retrieved her suitcase and they wheeled it into the office. The same puffy faced clerk wearing the glasses was there. They found out that in fact her grandma did need to sign a release for her to travel alone. The clerk assured her grandma that the driver would keep a watch over her during the trip. Her plan went off without a hitch, and she waved good bye to her grandma as she drove away. Chloe decided to stay in town until the bus departed just in case her grandma came back looking for her unexpectedly. She watched from a distance as the bus departed without her. Then when she decided all was safe, she began her walk back along the road while wheeling her suitcase in tow.

Before too long she came upon that pond and pulled her suitcase over the grass towards it in the shade. When she thought she was well concealed from the road behind a tree, she plopped the suitcase on its back and lay beside it. Earlier, while she was still in town she had bought a loaf of bread from the market to feed to the ducks, and was now throwing pieces to them. They all came over and swarmed around her as she fed them. After killing the whole day there among the ducks, it was starting to get dark and she decided it was time to get moving again.

In no time she was wheeling her suitcase up the driveway in the darkness. When she got near the front door, she looked up into the tree and saw Mr. Oppum waving to her. She waved back and proceeded to the front door. Just as she got there, she heard a fiddling of the lock from the inside. She quietly opened the door and saw Monty hopping back upstairs.

After closing the door, she stealthily followed him upstairs. Once she was again back with her friends at the center of Mr. Carpet, she whispered; "Hello everyone… I'm so excited I could explode! Are we ready for our journey?" Monty answered, "I do believe we are… but I am so nervous." Mr. Oppum jumped from his tree branch to the balcony and came into the room to join them. "Yes, it appears all is in order, let us take our seats and be off!"

Chloe brought her suitcase inside the tent, and after donning her heavy coat from it, she zipped it closed and pushed it to the rear. When she came back out she found that Mr. Oppum and Monty were sitting at the front and holding onto the rope. Monty looked at her as he raised his little arm to hand her something… it was the book of matches. She said;

"Oh yes, you are quite right… it would help if we could see where we are going." She took the matches, struck one, opened the little glass window of the lantern and lit it. Its mellow light cast a warm glow about the room. She closed it, put the matches into her coat pocket and sat beside them. They looked at one another, each seeing a look of apprehension mirrored back. Chloe looked around the room at all of her new friends.

"Well, wish us luck everyone!" There were whispered cheers about the room. Piano chimed softly,

"Oh, do please be safe…and come back in one piece!" Chest of drawers opened;

"Good luck!" Vacuum whirred;

"You will be in our prayers!" Wing back chair said;

"I wish I could go... please be safe..." And the wooden chair motioned;

"Farewell, my friends." Mr. Carpet flapped;

"Good bye all... until we meet again!"

At the back of the room a pair of green eyes emerged from the shadows... Rowena darted unnoticed to the rear of the tent where the chest was mounted. She quickly unlatched the lid, opened it and jumped inside to hide amongst the blankets and pillows. The lid closed noiselessly.

Just then, Chloe noticed all the edges of Mr. Carpet began to slightly flutter and vibrate...then, seemingly effortlessly, they arose magically from the attic floor and hovered there as light as a feather for a few moments. Chloe giggled excitedly... uncontrolledly,

"Here we go... I can't believe it...good bye all!" She waved good bye while holding tightly with her other hand. And then with their eyes wide...marveling...and the glow of the lantern lighting their way, they noiselessly drifted right out through the open French doors... rising higher as they proceeded past the balcony railing towards a full summer moon.

If one was standing outside below, they would be witness to the incredible sight of a magic carpet gliding across a full summer moon... carrying three impossible travelers guided by a lit brass lantern...and sitting before a camping tent and travelling chest.

Chapter 6

Chloe was glad that she had put on her coat, as it was getting chilly as they continued to rise ever higher towards some light misty clouds. She looked back whence they came and saw that the house was growing smaller and farther away. She could see everything clearly; the house, the barn, the river gorge and bridge were well lit by the full moon. It all looked …peaceful, and beautiful; surrounded by the vast evergreen forest. She said;

"Well, I thought I would be quite frightened by now, but actually I'm very much enjoying our ride."

"I am as well…this is very exciting," replied Mr. Oppum. Monty also added;

"Oh my friends…this is extraordinary, we are going to have the most astonishing adventure." Chloe ran her palm along Mr. Carpet and asked; "How are you doing Mr. Carpet?"

"Everything is perfect Chloe. At first I was worried about all of the weight, but it doesn't seem to make any difference at all." She again addressed him;

"You mentioned before that this journey had taken several days…"

"Yes, it did. We traveled mostly by the cover of night, I think it prudent we do the same this time as well. But when we are over the ocean it is not so important, as there are not many others around to notice us."

"Oh my… I hadn't thought of the ocean," Chloe said, worriedly.

After a time, Chloe decided she needed to do something to keep her hands busy. She stood and carefully made her way into the tent to fetch her tree branch and the knife they had brought. She was planning to work on it, so that is where she had stored them. She made her way back outside and again took her place. Monty and Mr. Oppum were looking on inquisitively.

"This will be my weapon, and in a little time, also my fashionable walking stick," she explained. With that, she began using the knife to cut off all of the little unwanted protruding bits, and the bark as well. At one end of it, there was a natural knobbiness which would do well as a possible handle. She took her time whittling away at it.

They all enjoyed the view as they floated onwards. Occasionally, they would see the lights of small towns in the distance, and then they would pass over them. The buildings, the moving traffic, and the people walking around were surreal. She knew that generally they were traveling eastward, and that they would be traversing the whole length of the country. She thought that the only cities that she might recognize would be Chicago, New York City, or Washington D.C. Even though she had never been to those places… they would probably be apparent to her…but those were still a long way off.

"I suppose we should start devising some sort of a plan on how to get the jewel back from Rajeem once we get there. As yet I haven't given it any thought," Chloe said.

"I haven't either," countered Monty, adding;

"Realistically, I don't think that we could until we at least get closer and see what we're up against."

"Yes, I think you are quite right," agreed Mr. Oppum. Chloe continued working on her staff as they drifted through the night. After a time she began to get sleepy and said;

"Well, I think I should lie down for a while in the tent, I'm getting a little tired." She looked down and noticed Monty was already napping by her side. Mr. Oppum then said;

"You go ahead then, I'll be here watching over things." She decided to take Monty with her into the tent as well, and gingerly picked him up in her free hand.

"Ok then, good night," she said as she made her way inside. She put her friend down onto a pillow that they had put in there and then lay down next to him to share it. She pulled a blanket over them both and easily drifted off to sleep. After a few hours, she and Monty awoke to the sound of Mr. Oppum calling out to them;

"Chloe...Monty..." She and Monty arose and looked out of the tent. It was beginning to be dawn, as it was getting a little brighter outside. Mr. Oppum said;

"Mr. Carpet and I think it is time that we should be setting down out of sight somewhere."

"Yes, you both are quite right," Chloe said as she and Monty reclaimed their seats to hold onto the rope. She noticed that they were headed towards a particular house.

"Surely we're not going to land in the back yard of that house are we?" Mr. Carpet answered;

"Yes, a friend lives there... I will elaborate more after we land."

They then set down by a tree in the middle of the yard. Rowena, still unnoticed by them, poked her head out of the chest to look around, then hopped out and disappeared into a nearby bush. Chloe was feeling a little nervous as she stood and walked over to a garden bench next to them and sat down, querying;

"So tell me, what friend could this possibly be?"

"Yes, do tell, I'm intrigued as well," Mr. Oppum also asked, as he and Monty joined her on the bench. Mr. Carpet began:

"We made good time last night and we are all the way across the country now in the state of Virginia. This house belongs to a friend and previous associate of your Grandpa Jack. We first came here after crossing the Atlantic Ocean from India those few years ago. It seems logical that we will be safe here, and also that we should inform him of our plans, as he was involved with the previous events as well. We spent a few days here as your Grandpa Jack and he spoke at great length about all that had transpired in India. His name is Mr. John Franks."

"Well, if you are sure, then I'm feeling a bit better about it now," Chloe replied.

She then noticed it was almost full morning now, as the sun had just risen. She looked around the yard and at the house. It was large and had two stories with a tall pitched wood shingled roof. There were many lead glass windows, and ivy had grown up around all of them. She thought she could faintly smell coffee brewing.

Just then, she saw movement at the window of the rear door. A curtain had pulled back and someone was looking out at them. Clearly she could see a look of astonishment flash across the man's face when he noticed them. He then immediately burst out of the door.

"Oh my stars, am I dreaming!?" He exclaimed, as he rushed over to them, adding;

"I don't believe it… Mr. Carpet… and you've brought friends!"

"Good morning John, nice to see you again. Yes I've brought friends…this is Chloe, she is Jacks granddaughter, and these two are Monty, and Mr. Oppum." They each nodded their heads in turn. "It's very nice to meet you all," he said.

"Likewise," they chimed in unison. He was a tall man with a thick head of gray-brown hair, hawkish features with a prominent nose, and friendly looking blue-gray eyes. He was wearing white pajamas and slippers under his navy blue bathrobe.

"But you must come inside and out of the cold… come along," he said, as he led the way. He opened some dual French doors so Mr. Carpet could fit in as well, and they all followed him inside.

Once they were inside he closed the doors, turned, and walked to a table nearby, saying;

"Come, sit and become comfortable. I will make you some hot cocoa to warm your bones." Chloe, Monty, and Mr. Oppum made their way to the table and sat down. They watched John prepare their drinks as he chatted with them;

"Oh my... Jacks granddaughter Chloe...and enchanted critters... this seems to be serious business!"

"I'm afraid it is. We're on a quest to regain the jewel if you haven't already guessed," Mr. Carpet flapped.

"I'm relieved to hear it to tell you the truth. I still have connections with Washington, and I'm hearing that the situation with the Maharaja Rajeem is again spinning out of control. No one in our government has believed me about the strange crystal that he had. After I told them about it, they thought that I was mad...and then they dismissed me of my post!"

"Lately, I've suspected that he again must have hold of it, because some situations around the world are echoing familiar troubles. Somehow, Rajeem is again regaining the unflappable obedience of his neighboring countries rulers', and I am afraid that it is only a matter of time before we will suffer the same fate! Imagine our whole country... The United States of America... under his control and all of us his slaves. Something must be done immediately!" Chloe decided it was time for her to speak up;

"Yes, we have also understood the importance of this situation, and also what a monumental task this is for us. You would be most welcome to come along and help us."

"I wish that I could, but I am in very poor health, and I'm afraid I would only be a hindrance to you," John answered.

"Oh that is too bad, and I'm sorry to hear that you are not well;" quipped Mr. Oppum. John continued, as he brought them their cocoa;

"But I have something that could very well help you..." With that, he walked past them, over Mr. Carpet, and out of the room. They heard him rifling through a drawer somewhere...and then he returned carrying a very small leather satchel. He sat at the table with them and explained;

"When Jack was last here, we spent time analyzing that jewel he had taken from Rajeem. We brought it to a gemologist and had a portion cut from it and faceted." John then opened the satchel and let an amethyst colored jewel spill out onto the white surface of the table.

They all sat transfixed... they couldn't take their eyes from its beautiful brilliance. It shone with its own internal glow. Chloe gasped;

"Look, something's happening to it!" They all watched with mouths agape as a beam of intense amethyst light shot out of it and onto the ceiling. Then the beam started wavering, and an eerie whining and humming sound began. They all simultaneously let out startled screams and quickly stood up as their chairs fell backwards onto the floor. John exclaimed;

"My god, this has never happened before!" Then the whole room began to vibrate and anything that was not fastened to the floor or a wall began to move around jerkily. They all dove for what cover they could find behind a counter that divided the kitchen and breakfast room.

They huddled there terrified, holding onto one another for a minute that seemed to last an hour as the sounds and vibrations intensified. And then as quickly as it had started...it stopped. They looked at one another with looks of mirrored confusion.

"I think it's safe to come out now..." said John.

They rose from the floor and peeked over and around the counter. The whole room was a complete and utter disheveled mess. Chloe said;

"I really can't imagine what that was all about... I'm still shaking... I need to sit down." She went over and pulled her chair up off of the floor and again sat at the table, which was a wet mess of spilled hot chocolate. Mr. Carpet flapped;

"Oh, I think I can feel what just happened, the same as happened to me long ago... I'm sure that before too long you are going to have a lot of company in this room." John asked,

"What do you mean?"

"I think he means that you will soon need to give names to all of your new friends in here... this table, these chairs...everything, Chloe said.

"I can now feel consciousness everywhere in this room, and they can now hear us as well, but it will be a while before they understand what is being said. And even longer before they can move and speak. That is what happened to me at least," Mr. Carpet said.

"Oh my goodness..." said John, as he mopped up the mess on the table with a dish towel while avoiding the gem. He felt timid about touching it just now. They all were again transfixed with it, not being able to tear their eyes from it. John continued;

"When the gemologist studied it, he said he found that it had some unexplainable properties, such as a small electrical charge...that would increase when touched. And also that some sounds would sometimes emanate from it."

"It really is beautiful... isn't it?" Chloe said, as she timidly poked it with her finger. It seemed safe now to touch it, so she picked it up and held it in her palm while ogling it.

"I can't help but wonder what else it's capable of doing..." she looked at Jack, continuing;

"So you think it would be a good idea to take it with us...I agree, it may ultimately help us somehow. Maybe we will eventually learn how to harness some of its powers to use against the Maharaja." John countered;

"Yes, I definitely think that you should take it, but I'm also concerned that it's rather easy to be misplaced by dropping it... it needs to be affixed to something."

"You are right, I have just the thing to fasten it to!" She said, and set it again onto the table and ran out the back door, and after a moment she returned with her whittled staff. During the previous evening, she had finished carving it. She set it upon the table next to the gem. Mr. Oppum said;

"Yes, that is the perfect object to mount it to." John picked it up and inspected it.

"I agree...let us take it into my work shop out back and see what we can do." He collected the jewel as well and they all followed him out back. Chloe said on her way out;

"We'll see you in a little while Mr. Carpet."

He led them on a little path through his garden towards the garage and they followed him into its' side door. He turned on the light and went to a work bench as they gathered around. Monty and Mr. Oppum found their way onto its surface to watch. John set the items upon the bench.

"Now let us see what we can do with these," he said as he pondered a moment while scratching his chin. He had many tools neatly organized along the back board. He pulled a small box out of a drawer and opened it. After fishing through it, he held up a gold chain with a pendant that contained on old opal.

"This was one of my late wife's many pieces of jewelry; I do think that she would approve of us using it." He removed the pendant from the chain.

After finding a pair of needle nose pliers from the board, he carefully removed the opal. He then held their jewel to the setting...it looked roughly around the same size.

"I think with a little finagling it will serve our purpose," he said. They all watched interestedly. He mounted the jewel into the setting, then picked up the staff, and held their jewel against the top of the staff.

"I think mounting it right onto the top would be all right...." He then found a small knife and carved an indentation into the top of the staff. The jewel was about three quarters of an inch in diameter, shaped in an octagon fashion. After perfectly carving the wood, he set the mounted jewel into the indentation. It fit perfectly snug. "Yes I believe that will do," he said, then put the jewel back onto the bench.

"I think we should finish this staff a little more first." With that, he pulled out a piece of sand paper, and for a few minutes, rubbed the entire surface of the wood, stopping periodically to test the smoothness of it. When he felt that it was enough, he put away the sand paper.

"It's looking a little too bare I think," he said, and then went to a cabinet and pulled out a can of something and brought it back and opened it.

"This is a wood stain; it will make it look much less bare and pale looking." He found a brush and used it to coat the staff with the stain, then; using a rag he wiped it dry. The wood looked quite striking; one could see all the interesting grains in it. He then took a piece of string and tacked it to the bottom of the staff, and hung it upside down from a hook on the low ceiling. Then, again he went to the cabinet and brought back a spray can of something.

"This is a finish spray," he said, as he lightly sprayed the whole surface of the staff. He then plugged in an electric fan and directed it towards it.

"We will wait a few minutes for it to dry," he said.

Then, after a short time, he touched it.

"Yes, it feels dry now." He then pulled the string off of the staff and studied it for a moment.

"My, it looks pretty... and shiny too," Chloe said.

"Ok, it's ready for the jewel now," he said, and then set the jewel into the indentation he had carved into the handle after first applying a small amount of very strong glue.

"Well; it was a little work... but I do believe it is finished now," he said, as he held it out for all to see. They all gave a little applause. "Here you are Chloe," he said, as he handed it to her.

She reached out her hand and said "Thank you John," and grasped it. Suddenly, a jolting shock of electricity traveled the length of her body...she was paralyzed. Her eyes widened as she loudly screamed out in pain. There was a strong smell of ozone as a whoosh of hot air and a thick violet mist quickly enveloped her. She felt completely disoriented...as if she were no longer in the work shop.

The paralyzing pang then began to be accompanied with charged energy bolts of amethyst plasma shooting from her body in all directions. The roar of the wind and crackling energy were deafening. Suddenly, as if she hadn't felt frightened enough, she was beginning to somehow detect another presence with her somewhere there in the mist. It was an increasing feeling of dark dread, like death, and it sickened her stomach.

She still could not move... and then she saw it... just before her, a large black eye began to materialize. It peered at her intensely, scrutinizing and narrowing. Then suddenly... she didn't know how...but she felt within her some knowledge to channel all of the energy crackling around her body, and quickly grasped the staff in both hands and pointed it towards the eye.

The amethyst plasma coalesced and shot out of her jeweled staff towards it. The eye widened in surprised terror... then ran red with blood as the amethyst bolts struck it. A loud deafening scream of pain mixed with rage rang out echoingly... and then quickly faded away along with the terrifying vision. She lowered her arms, suddenly feeling exhausted. The windy mist immediately evaporated, and was replaced with the scene of the workshop. Her three friends were standing there aghast, helplessly holding onto one another.

"Chloe... are you alright!?" they all asked in unison. She stood there a moment staring at them. Then suddenly, she felt dizzy and weak. Dropping the staff and crumpling to the floor, she fell into unconsciousness. They rushed to her. Monty stood next to her face and exclaimed; "She's still breathing!" Mr. Oppum ordered;

"Quickly, let's get her into the house." John then scooped her up and they made their way through the yard and into the house. Mr. Carpet fluttered;

"I heard that scream... what is wrong with Chloe!?" John then placed her on a couch and laid her head onto a pillow and said; "She is still breathing..."

After a few minutes she began to come to. Her eyes opened and she saw all of them gathered around her. John was holding her hand. She sat up startled, saying;

"Oh my gosh, I saw him... he was looking at me with that black eye..." She then relayed to them what had happened to her in the mist. Monty told her;

"We couldn't see any of that. All that we could see was that cloud with violet colored bolts of lightning shooting out in all directions, but we could hear everything." John added;

"Yes...that scream was terrifying...it rattled the fillings in my teeth it was so loud. I wouldn't be surprised if the police were to show up now."

"Well, it seems we have learned a few things… that the jeweled staff has proven itself a formidable weapon…and also unfortunately we may have spoiled our element of surprise," John said.

"Yes, on both of those counts you are most certainly correct. I can't help but wonder if my encounter with him has truly wounded him in any significant way," Chloe replied.

"Well, we could hope that the answer to that would be yes. But losing our element of surprise is a most disastrous circumstance for us. We will now have to be continually on our guard from now on," Mr. Carpet added, followed by Mr. Oppum;

"All the more reason that I think we now should probably get there as soon as possible. He must know that we are still quite a long distance away from him, and we don't want to give him any more time than necessary to prepare against us."

"Yes, quite right. We should leave immediately," said Monty.

With that said they quickly gathered their things. John suggested that they should take some food with them from his pantry, and while they were all distracted in the kitchen and making noise, Rowena again made her way quickly back into the chest to hide, being careful not to lay a paw onto Mr. Carpet. They then all made their way back into the room, and after quickly adding the new food items into the chest, (they haphazardly tossed them into the chest, pummeling Rowena on her head with heavy canned goods as she cursed and swore at them to herself under a thin blanket) they pronounced themselves ready to disembark.

"I will be praying for your success and safe return," John said to all of them. They exchanged handshakes and hugs. Chloe, Monty, and Mr. Oppum again took their places at the front of Mr. Carpet, sitting and holding onto their rope. Chloe, holding onto her staff with her free hand, raised it in salute to John and said;

"Untill we meet again!" And with that, they rose off the floor, circled the room, and floated out of the open French doors into the night.

Chapter 7

After rising above the house, the four travelers again continued east. Chloe decided to keep her staff in close proximity in case they needed it for protection, so she reached behind her and placed it into their tent. After a long while the vast forests of Virginia gave way to the city lights of dense civilization. It then got denser still when they came to what could only be New York City.

They were already traveling at quite a high altitude, but the buildings that they were approaching would be surpassing even their height. Chloe said;

"Oh my… it looks as though we are going to be flying into and between all of those buildings!" Mr. Carpet replied;

"Yes, I think it may be too dangerous for us to fly over them, or we risk being struck by an airplane." Mr. Oppum countered;

"Yes, quite right. That would be most disagreeable."

"Well, we can only hope that we are not seen by anyone inside the buildings as we pass by," said Chloe.

They then began passing right through the heart of the city. It was very bright there, and Chloe knew they must have been plainly visible to anyone who looked their way. Mr. Carpet said;

"I will speed up to make this as quick as possible." They all whooped and hollered as if on an amusement park ride while they zigzagged around the buildings. Then, as they passed the roof top of one of them, they noticed that a helicopter was taking off relatively close to them, and also that it was a local television news vehicle.

"Oh my goodness… I think that we have been spotted… look, I can see them inside of it… and they're pointing at us!" Chloe exclaimed, and added; "They're following us, we must shake them… or we will be on television!" Mr. Carpet said; "Hold on, I will try!"

They quickly veered right… circling around what Chloe thought looked very much like the Empire State building…then shot like a cannon ball straight ahead for a distance through the sky maze. They then came out into a clearing with many bright animated digital signs.

"Oh no, we're now in Times Square… we really must leave this city now!" Chloe said, while pointing ahead and added;

"Look, see that statue off in the distance? We must head in that direction, I'm sure it will take us out over the ocean."

"Yes, I recognize that," said Mr. Carpet, as he then doubled their speed. They all held on more tightly as the wind buffeted their ears. Chloe caught a glimpse of her reflection in a mirrored glass window as they rocketed past, she thought her hair looked like flowing red neon in the light. The helicopter was nowhere to be seen as they approached the huge green statue.

"Yay... it's the Statue of Liberty!" Chloe yelled, as they passed between the arm holding the torch and its' crowned head. She added;

"I shall never forget this moment.... Incredible!" They then shot out over the ocean. Mr. Carpet then slowed down considerably to a more comfortable speed. They all turned, peering around the tent to watch the city lights recede. It was all very peaceful now... and quiet, accompanied by fairy light stars and a cool breeze. The moon shone brightly and was also reflected in the ocean below them.

After a time, Monty rubbed his little belly, saying;

"I do believe it must be past my dinner time... I'm famished" "Oh, I am as well," commiserated Mr. Oppum.

"I will get us something to eat from the chest," Chloe said as she carefully made her way to the chest. From the inside of it, Rowena heard them speak of it and burrowed herself deeper out of sight. Chloe opened it and grabbed some canned goods, a can opener, and a bottle of grape juice, and returned to the front and sat with the others. She set them in her lap as she decided to first relight their brass lantern.

After fishing the matches out of her pocket and lighting it, she then opened the cans of split pea soup and hung them on the little open door of the brass lamp to let them warm for a time. In short order they were all enjoying their warm soup, followed by cans of fruit cocktail.

"Well, that was satisfying, but I think a good night's sleep is in order, I'm going to bed… good night all," Chloe said, as she made her way into the tent. Monty again joined her, and before long they both were snuggled up comfortably and sawing logs.

When Chloe awoke the next morning and came out of the tent, she noticed in the predawn light that they were approaching land. "My, have we already crossed the entire Atlantic ocean?" she asked as she sat down.

"Yes, we certainly have. I will bring us down as soon as possible," answered Mr. Carpet. When they reached the shore, the sun was just peeking over the horizon. They travelled on for just a few minutes more to find a secluded place, and landed in a field of grass and trees at the edge of a quaint looking medieval town of stone buildings and cottages. Once on the ground Mr. Carpet said;

"I think this is a good spot to stay hidden." Chloe looked around, commenting; "I wonder what country we are in… I would like very much to explore the little town for a while."

"Oh, please take me with you!" exclaimed Monty.

"Ok… maybe you would be comfortable in my shirt pocket. I don't think that you would attract much attention in there, as you would only look like my little pet."

"That sounds like fun," he said, as Chloe picked him up and put him in her pocket.

"Ok, you two go explore and please be careful, in the meanwhile I will get some sleep," Mr. Oppum said, and then proceeded to climb up the tree right next to them.

Chloe walked to the road and followed it in the direction that she had seen the town, and after a short time they rounded a bend in the road and there it was. She noticed there were a few villagers going about their morning business walking to and fro.

As she walked, she fell in love with this charming little picturesque town. They came upon a little café beside the cobble stone street upon which they were walking. There was a man sitting at one of its tables on the sidewalk, reading his paper and smoking a pipe. He looked up at them as she approached.

"Bon jour," he said.

"Bon jour," she replied. Well, that answered her question as to where they were, anyway… they were in France. She decided to take a seat at one of the tables to relax. Almost immediately a friendly looking, motherly woman came out.

"Bon Jour Mademoiselle," she said as she handed her a little menu. "Bon jour… do you speak English?" she asked.

"Oui, oui… yes, I do. What may I get for you?"

"I think I would like a hot cocoa and a pastry please."

"Of course… I will be back shortly," she said, and went back inside.

She then noticed the man was smiling at her as he looked at Monty inside her pocket and back to her once again. She smiled back at him and nodded her head, and he nodded back. After a short time the waitress returned with her treat and set it down in front of her, then busily made her way back inside. Chloe portioned off a little of her pastry onto a napkin and let Monty crawl down her arm onto the table to join her in her breakfast.

While she luxuriated, taking in the sight of the little town and enjoying her exquisite pastry, she happened to glance at the cover page of the newspaper that the man had his head buried in. Interestingly, she saw the word India in the title of the lead story, and accompanying it was a large photo of who most probably was the Maharaja Rajeem. He was wearing a turban on his head which was adorned with a large jewel… 'The' jewel of course! Chloe covertly gained Monty's attention and directed it towards the paper. His little eyes widened in surprise as he noticed it.

Chloe spoke to the man;

"Excuse me sir, do you speak English?" He closed his paper, answering;

"Yes, I do. How may I help you Mademoiselle?"

"Could you please tell me what that article on the front page about India is all about?"

"Why yes…but I'm not sure I understand it completely. It seems the Maharaja Rajeem of India is now our new president. But it makes no sense to me, as this is the country of France and therefore that would be impossible… I am shocked and outraged… and honestly not a little frightened about it!"

Just then there was the sound of someone's scream and the breaking of some china inside the café. Chloe, Monty and the man immediately stood up and ducked inside to see what had happened.

There were a few customers sitting at different tables, along with the waitress standing there with broken china at her feet. They all were staring upwards at a television mounted on the wall. The scene there was almost indescribable…it seemed to be a news broadcast from Paris; its streets were choked with protesters. The camera was focused on the Eiffel Tower, and above it was a compact cloud of an amethyst colored mist.

There was no mistaking the impossible image of a large eye peering out of it. And there was the sound of the news caster rapidly relaying the events in the background. Then suddenly the cloud erupted with violet colored lightning bolts which were directed at the tower, accompanied with a thunderous booming. The bolts themselves also made their own crackling sounds as they continuously pelted the tower.

Chloe watched in horror… she could see that there were many people in the tower, which began to start glowing orange within the heat and black smoke. Then impossibly… the whole structure began to warp, it sagged to the right. The sounds of screaming could be heard from the populous of the onlookers as they ran in all directions in a fit of terror. In the café, they all gasped and screamed uncontrollably as they watched.

Chloe could also hear the same thing trough out the village outside, as many also must have been watching the broadcast. They couldn't take their eyes off of the television, and as they stared at the screen they watched as the tower got hotter still, and the orange glow began to change into a more orange-red… then it happened. The structure began to melt to the ground in flames. In the space of ten minutes there was nothing left but a pool of molten steel covering a large area of the ground… there was a lot of black smoke billowing off of it. The bolts then ceased and the cloud just dispersed as if it had never been there.

Chloe had seen enough, she staggered shakily out of the café. She saw other town's people had also emerged outside; there was a general sense of panic as they formed in groups… talking excitedly and gesticulating. Monty was still in her pocket; they eyed one another but couldn't find any words to convey what they felt. Chloe sat at her table…feeling a little sick. She sat there for a while, not knowing what to do with herself as she watched the others come out of the café to converse with a nearby group. She decided that she needed to hear what they were saying, maybe someone could translate for her, and so with Monty in her shirt pocket she ventured a little closer to the group. After standing there for a few minutes she noticed that there was a little boy around her age sitting on the small rock wall that formed the perimeter of the café patio. He also noticed her at the same time.

He smiled shyly when he saw her and Monty. He was wearing a charming little worn dark blue vest with matching draw string cotton pants, with an off white long sleeved shirt. On his head he wore the typical French cap in beige and brown knit. His face looked a little dirty and she got the impression that he might be from an orphanage nearby. She timidly made her way over to him and said;

"Hello, my name is Chloe, I'm an American. Do you speak English?" He again smiled at her and Monty and replied;

"Why, yes I do…I have been practicing a lot lately. My name is Honore', but you can call me Onri, I'm glad to make your acquaintance." Chloe asked him;

"Are your parents out here as well?"

"Ah no… I no longer have any family. Are you visiting here with yours?" She then answered;

"I am here with my friends only…did you see on TV what happened?"

"Yes I did…it is truly frightening and also just completely unbelievable." Chloe thought for a moment, and further asked;

"Do you think it has anything to do with your new president the Maharaja Rajeem?"

"That is generally what everyone out here is talking about. There were some strange things that happened in the recent past concerning that man from India."

"Once before he had proclaimed himself our president…and shortly afterwards our own president mysteriously vanished. Some said they witnessed him…our president…swallowed up in a strange kind of eerie purple mist. Then the Maharaja was our president for a few months. There were many protests in the streets by our citizens, and many of them vanished into that same mist, at least that is what people said they saw happen." Chloe listened to him and thought that he might be willing to help them in their quest… he seemed a genuinely trustworthy and nice little boy.

"Onri, I wonder if you would be willing to help me. I am here with my friends for the very reason of vanquishing that man… but it is such a monumental task, and without a doubt a very dangerous one at that." Onri's eyes perked up upon hearing this.

"That is my one wish right now… you see, my parents were with one of those protest groups in Paris before, and now they are gone…" Chloe was startled to hear this. She felt bad for him, for she also knew how terrible it is to lose ones parents in a tragedy.

"Onri, I have a huge secret to share with you. Would you like to come with me to meet my friends?"

"Yes Chloe, I would like that very much!"

"Great… then let us go now." She paid her bill at the table, and then led him away from the café along the cobble stone street which turned back into a dirt lane at the edge of town.

"You know, Onri, the first friend of mine that I'd like you to meet is walking with us right now…" With a surprised look, Onri looked around them and saw no one.

"Chloe, you're teasing me. There's no one here with us…"

"But you are wrong; Monty is here with us now." She looked at Monty in her pocket.

"But that is only your pet mouse." Monty interjected;

"I beg your pardon sir, but I am not a pet. It's nice to make your acquaintance Mr. Onri." Onri jumped away in surprise and stood staring… dumbfounded.

"Did that little mouse just speak to me!?" Chloe answered;

"Yes, as impossible as it may seem he did just that."

"But how… I don't understand…"

"I'm afraid that shortly you will have more surprises… it's best to keep an open mind from now on."

"I see… well then… it's nice to meet you Mr. Monty the mouse." "Likewise, I hope I didn't startle you too much." They continued walking. After passing a bend in the road, Chloe led him between a break in the low rock wall that bordered the road and past some small trees and bushes to the clearing where her compatriots were waiting. Chloe said;

"Onri, my other two friends are also enchanted surprises. This is Mr. Magic Carpet." She waved her hand to introduce him to a carpet on the ground. He looked at it, with its' tent and chest upon it, thinking how strange it looked sitting here in a field. He said;

"But surly… a carpet could not be your friend." Mr. Carpet then flapped;

"It's nice to meet you Mr. Onri." Again Onri was taken by surprise. He didn't know what to say,

"I have never spoken to a carpet before… I'm afraid I will feel myself mad if I do… hello." Chloe then said;

"And lastly, we have Mr. Oppum... Mr. Oppum!" she called up into the tree. Onri looked up, and on a branch hanging upside down, and snoring quite loudly, was an opossum. Chloe again called; "Mr. Oppum, wake up, we have a new friend for you to meet!" Mr. Oppum's snoring ceased in a few funny snorts and his eyes opened. "Huh...? ... Oh... forgive me," he said, and swung upwards to sit upon his branch. He continued;

"Hello sir, I'm Mr. Oppum. Please excuse me, as I did not catch your name." Onri thought it funny to hear an opossum speaking to him with an impeccably perfect British accent.

"Ha ha... I'm Onri, nice to make your acquaintance." Mr. Oppum climbed down to the ground at his feet and held out a paw to him. Onri shook it with his fingers.

Chloe motioned for Onri to sit with her on Mr. Carpet;

"Please have a seat; I'm afraid we have much to catch you up on. I will make us some hot cocoa...I got distracted at the café and didn't get to finish my earlier one." Onri sat down. He watched Chloe busy herself with lighting the brass lamp to heat up their drinks.

All the while he listened to her miraculous tale of their friends back home, her family and the jewel, and their journey to this place. When Chloe reached the end of their tale thus far, they had finished their drinks. All the while Onri had sat quietly, wide eyed, and slack jawed. He then asked her;

"May I see this magic jeweled staff of yours? I promise to be careful with it."

"Certainly," she answered, as she leaned back and reached into the tent. She pulled it out and handed it to him.

"Wow…" he marveled, as he ran his hands over it, feeling its smooth finished surface. He then looked at the amethyst-like jewel on its handle. When the internal light of it caught his eyes, he sighed uncontrolledly. He couldn't help but gaze closely into its depths… deeper… deeper still.

He felt frozen. The muscles in his arm, shoulder, and neck suddenly began to ache… he truly could not move them if he tried. Then he saw something begin to stir inside the jewel… like a swirling pattern. A cold sweat broke out upon his forehead and he began to panic. He screamed; "Chloe, help… I can't move! Something is happening!"

He still couldn't take his eyes off of the jewel. He felt as though his vision was being drawn inside of it…and then 'he' was inside of it! He looked to the right, to the left, and all around. It was a terrifyingly beautiful world of glowing, deep purple facets…and there were sounds…like echoing whispers of different kinds, coming from all different directions.

He began to feel disoriented as he noticed a light colored violet mist stirring at the edges of all of the facets, mirrored and gradually shifting like the inside of a kaleidoscope. He then began to feel as though he were getting permanently trapped inside of it! He screamed for help again, but he couldn't tell if anyone could hear him; as his voice sounded very thin and didn't seem to travel anywhere. Then to his utter amazement, he began to realize that all of those whispering sounds he was hearing were actually human voices.

He strained to listen more closely… there were hundreds of them… could his mother and father be trapped in here? His heart skipped a beat at the thought of that possibility. He called out; "Mummy… Daddy…! Then, impossibly, he thought he could hear some far away answer; "Onri, it's us, we're here, can you hear me?"

Just then he felt a painful jolt of electricity shock his entire being and he felt his consciousness quickly fade away.

After a time, he began to wake up and he opened his eyes. He was lying on his back outside somewhere under a tree… and someone was sitting next to him and looking down at his face. She was calling his name;

"Onri… Onri…wake up." He then got his wits about him, remembered everything and sat up. He felt dizzy and a little sick to his stomach. He said;

"Chloe…Monty…Mr. Oppum…Mr. Carpet…I'm back!" Chloe answered;

"But you never went anywhere…you sat there frozen for a few moments while looking into the jewel and calling to us for help. Then when I shook your shoulder you momentarily collapsed into unconsciousness. Do you remember what happened?"

"Yes, I felt as if I were trapped inside a kind of purple prism, then there was a mist…and I could hear many whispering voices…sad, lost voices calling out. But I couldn't see anyone. Oh, now I remember…I called out to my mom and dad…I could feel them there somewhere…Chloe, they answered me!" He buried his face into his hands and began to sob uncontrolledly,

"Oh my god…I pray they are still alive. We must find them!"

Chloe, Monty, and Mr. Oppum looked at one another in shock. Chloe said;

"Onri, if it is in our power, I promise you that we will find them...we must...and all the rest of those trapped people, if in fact that is what you found. We are learning new things about this whole situation as we go along. We will get to the bottom of it!" Onri looked up from his wet hands. His puffy, red tearstained face brightened upon hearing her convictions.

Then suddenly he felt anger, then rage. He stood up,

"There is not a moment to lose; we must find that evil man. And we must kill him!" Chloe was not surprised he felt this way, she imagined that she would as well. He continued;

"I need a weapon, I have my families' ancestral sword hidden in the nearby forest where I have been living...like an animal because of him. I will be back shortly." He then bounded off, disappearing through the brush. Chloe said; "He is certainly right about one thing, there is not a moment to lose." And with that, she began making ready to depart.

A short time later, Onri returned holding what was certainly his afore mentioned sword. He said;

"I see we are ready to leave, as everything is tidily stowed." Chloe answered;

"Yes, as soon as you are ready we can depart."

"Then let us make haste." Chloe sat first and motioned;

"Onri, please be seated here next to me, and pull this rope over your folded legs so that you can hold onto it." He then sat next to her, followed by Monty and Mr. Oppum. Onri felt completely perplexed and asked;

"But Chloe, how can we travel anywhere by just sitting here?" She answered;

"Now don't be frightened, but this is actually a magic flying carpet, and quite a one fun!" Mr. Carpet then announced;

"Ok, fasten your seat belts...oh, we don't have any, well you know what I mean...here we go!" Onri sat there wide eyed as he looked down at Mr. Carpet and noticed all of his edges begin to slightly flutter. Then, true to Chloe's word, they slowly rose upward off of the ground while rotating to face an easterly direction. Onri giggled loudly as it greatly tickled his stomach. He exclaimed;

"Wow...I've never even flown in an airplane before, much less a magic carpet...wee!" They circled the area once they reached their cruising height. They all could see the little village as they looked down. Chloe said;

"Until now we have only been flying under the cover of night, but I don't think that we have the luxury any longer of waiting until then." Onri answered;

"Yes, I think that you're right." They then proceeded towards the east and in no time they were traveling quite fast. Chloe then asked;

"May I see your sword, Onri?"

"Yes" he answered, as he unsheathed it, saying;

"This is all that I have left of my family's belongings, it is very old. My father said it belonged to his great, great grandfather. He was a soldier in a time when men rode horse back to protect their king and country. It seems it is now my turn, except my horse has been replaced by a magic carpet... ha ha!" He held it in both hands to display it for her to see.

Chloe thought it looked exquisite. The long steel blade looked very sharp. She noticed that there were runes engraved all along it, and at the hilt of it was a family coat of arms. Parts of the handle were made of gold and intricately casted with great detail.

"It chills me to think of you having to use that, but unfortunately you may just have to before this is all said and done." He answered;

"Well, at least I have had much practice in wielding it, as it has always been my favorite possession." He then returned his sword to its sheath and placed it into the tent behind them. They were quiet for a time while watching the passing countryside below. They noticed a farmer and his small herd of cattle all staring with mouths agape as they flew by. The farmer took off his hat and held it above his face to shield the sun as he watched them. He waved to them, and he saw them all wave back in return as they faded from view over a hill.

Chapter 8

Chloe found good company with all of her new friends as they surveyed the beauty of the passing French countryside. Occasionally they would pass a small village here and there. When about two hours were spent, Onri said;

"See that river in the distance to our right? It is the river Seine. If we should want to pass over Paris, then we only need follow it." Chloe answered;

"I think I am a little afraid to pass over that city after what has happened, but it may be necessary for us to get a full perspective of current affairs…what do you think?"

"Yes, I think that we should. It can't be too far from here, maybe a little ways past those hills in the distance." Mr. Carpet then began following the Seine, and when an hour had passed they were leaving those hills behind them when Chloe raised her arm to point ahead.

"I think I see it!" Onri looked, replying;

"Yes, we are almost there." The rural landscape began to give way to the density of small towns and streets. Chloe thought it seemed eerily quiet as they passed over. Surely there would normally be more traffic and people about, as it was only late afternoon.

Then almost at once they were approaching the city of Paris. As they arrived Chloe marveled at its beauty…the bridges over the Seine, the architecture of all the well preserved old buildings. But it too was just as quiet, something was definitely wrong. It was Onris' turn to point out;

"My god; that is where the Eiffel Tower should be…" Mr. Carpet headed in that direction, and as they approached, Chloe could indeed see in person what she had witnessed on the television. The only thing left of it was a huge molten heap of blackened steel. The area was not so quiet though. There were many people seemingly in mourning for those that were lost in the destruction, as most were weeping and sitting among piles of flowers that were brought. As they passed and continued on, it became very quiet again. Chloe lamented;

"Everyone must be shutting themselves in at home, in shock and afraid to come outside…and look at all of the empty cars on the streets with their doors left open, like they got stuck in traffic jams and had to flee suddenly." Onri agreed;

"Yes, that appears to be what has happened." Mr. Oppum motioned;

"Look over that way, something is happening…I think I see a large crowd of people!"

As they approached, they noticed that there were many military vehicles spread about…tanks, and Humvees. But they were all damaged and inoperable. Most were burned and seemingly partially molten…like the tower. What they saw next was chaotic and confusing. Mr. Carpet halted their advance and hovered in place as they watched.

There was much noise and commotion as a large crowd of protesters holding signs and chanting seemed to be being held together in tight quarters. Within the crowds perimeter people were in a panic and fighting those that were holding them there. But there were no people holding them there, only piles of everyday objects.

There were lawnmowers, garbage cans, furniture, bicycles, food carts, and anything one could think of. Chloe said;

"All of those things are alive and fighting to hold those people there… look!"

"Incredible!" replied Onri.

"What do the signs say that some of the people are holding, I can't read French."

"Let me see… 'Death to Rajeem',' kill the murderer.'" Just then a news media van rushed to the scene and stopped nearby. A man with a T.V. camera got out followed by a female news caster with long dark hair. She was holding and speaking into a microphone. They were filming the crowd. Then things began to turn more ominous. There was a crack of violet lightning that hit the center of the crowd from a lone violet colored cloud, followed by a boom of thunder. The mood of the crowd then became more frenzied as they all pushed to get away, but they were held fast.

Then it began…an amethyst mist started to materialize beyond the crowd, near the buildings across the street. There were many screams of terror when those in the crowd noticed it. The mist grew larger and less opaque…then started to move closer to the crowd. Chloe could see an image forming in it. It was a mouth…and it was opening as if to devour them all whole! She said;

"We must do something…quick, Mr. Carpet bring us to those things holding them there!" They flew directly to the objects. "Onri, use your sword on them, maybe you can break an opening for them to get away!"

Onri unsheathed his sword and it rang out as he vengefully struck a television, which smashed and shattered in a spray of wood and glass. Next was a tin trash can that crumpled and was flung aside, followed by the halving of a wooden book case. There was a cheer from the crowd as their path to escape broke open and they spilled forth. The terrified looks on their faces mixed with wonder as they passed their saviors.

Onri kept up his fight as the crowd tried to rush out, but Chloe gasped in horror as she saw the mist reach the far edge of the crowd…most of them were not going to escape! She ordered;

"Mr. Carpet, take us there!" She pointed with her staff. They rose above the crowd and advanced on the mist. Chloe stood up, and with one hand aiming the staff to the mist and the other holding onto the rope, she again began to feel that same surge of electricity as before when she last confronted this adversary.

Violet bolts of spider web like energy surrounded her body, shooting in all directions. Mr. Oppum and Monty dove for cover into the tent and Onri stooped down to avoid its melee. Chloe screamed; "Take us into the mouth!" Mr. Carpet complied and they shot as quickly as an arrow straight into it, disappearing from view.

When they got inside, it was the same as onri had
described it from earlier... all a depth of deep purple
crystal. There was no telling which way was up or down.
Mr. Carpet quickly lost his sense of navigation and
immediately they fell the short distance to the floor of it.
The jolt of it knocked Chloe and Onri off to the side. The

chest which was mounted onto the back sprang open and ejected all of its contents, including Rowena, who screeched as she flew into the air and landed with a thud on her back. Chloe aimed her staff at her when they both locked eyes in surprise. A single bolt of lightning cracked forth from it towards Rowena's posterior. She again screeched and managed to run away with a singed and smoking bottom, disappearing into the facets.

Monty and Mr. Oppum emerged shaken from the tent and joined Chloe and Onri. They stood there feeling disoriented. Chloe thought that she felt like an animal might feel when it's trapped, she also felt inconceivably small, lost in an endless void of nothing but intangible violet prisms. Then as Onri had spoken of before, there was again a mist forming at the mirrored edges of all of the crystal facets, which began to twirl in a dizzying kaleidoscope like dance.

They all held onto one another lest they fall disoriented to the ground. Then the whispers began… wails of lost torment and pain. They echoed and bounced thinly to and fro. Hundreds of them! When she spoke, it sounded tinny and seemed to hardly travel past her lips;

"This death trap must be destroyed. Everyone… get behind me, I can feel the energy of the staff building up again!" They ducked behind her near the tent a few feet back. Chloe held the staff horizontally above her head in both hands. Again violet colored energy crackled around her entire body accompanied with a tangy odor of ozone. Seemingly in response, the kaleidoscope of dizzying facets began spinning out of control all around them.

Chloe knelt on one knee to brace herself, and aimed her staff into the swirling void. She felt the energy channel through her and out of the staff. A thick bolt of violet plasma shot forth with a deafening crack as it hit the wall of the prism which then became discernible with that added point of reference. The flow of energy continued for a few moments as it soaked into the crystal…producing an undulating and whining sound. Defective fissures began to appear and expand rapidly. Suddenly, it looked as if it would all explode… and then it did just that!

With a deafening sound of shattering glass, the whole structure surrounding them burst outwards revealing the sky above. They were again standing on the street as millions of amethyst crystal shards fell all around them. They knelt and cowered there, shielding their heads. Then as it abated, they noticed that they were not alone…the multitudes that were trapped within it were standing all around them. There were cries of surprise and recognition from many people in the outside crowd as they spotted and called out to some of their lost loved ones that they thought would never be seen again.

There were joyous cheers as the crowds merged. Chloe and company were jostled about in the center of it all. Then Onri caught sight of his parents…he called out;

"Mummy…Daddy!" They then saw him and rushed over through the crowd. There they hugged and cried sobbingly for a good few minutes. Then, Chloe saw the television news anchor woman and camera man trying to make their way over to them through the crowd. She said to her cohorts;

"Everyone…quickly get onto Mr. Carpet, here comes' the news media!" They all jumped on as Onri pulled his unsuspecting parents on as well. Mr. Carpet rose above the crowd; which cheered in wonderment at them. Cries of thanks echoed the streets as they all waved and jumped about in excitement.

Chloe could see the news camera man catching them on film as his female coworker narrated. She said;

"Well, so much for our secret mission. Soon the whole world will be aware of us. I wonder if I was close enough to the camera to be recognizable to my family. I guess I won't know until I get back home…"

Mr. Carpet took them a distance away. They crossed the Seine and landed in a small deserted park. Onri introduced his parents, who stood in wide eyed disbelief. Chloe said;

"I'm delighted to make your acquaintance, I'm sorry…I only speak English" Onri's father answered;

"That is quite alright, we can understand you. I don't know how you accomplished such a feat…but we both thank you all from the bottom of our hearts!" Onri and his parents stepped to the side to continue their joyous reunion with a little more privacy. Chloe then said to her companions;

"I think we could use some well-deserved rest."

"I concur," replied Mr. Oppum, as he plopped his tired body into the tent and onto a pillow.

"Good idea," said Monty, as he sat down on Mr. Carpet.

"I think we all could use something to drink…I think something stronger that cocoa is in order. I know we acquired some coffee from John's pantry, let me see if we haven't lost it," Chloe replied, as she rummaged through the chest. After finding it she busied herself with the making of it, and before long they were all sitting and enjoying a cup. There was much to talk about what had happened, and what their plans were to be going forward.

Back across the river, amongst the thinning crowd and all of the shards of broken crystal, Rowena sat on the side walk near the opening of an alley, licking her wounds. She was in a foul mood, as things were not looking so good at the moment. The fur was singed off of her posterior, and it smarted as well…and she had also suffered a humiliating defeat.

"Well," she thought, "There is time to get even with them soon enough." As she sat there contemplating her next move, a smallish shard of crystal which was lying next to her caught her eye. She saw that an eye was looking out of it at her. She stopped licking her paw and stared at it…she knew that it was her master. His voice then emanated from it;

"I recognize you my loyal pet…though I've never had a name for you. What do you call yourself?" She answered; "I'm Rowena, my master. I'm glad to see that you are well. How can I be of assistance to you?"

"I know that you have been serving me well these many months, and I thank you. I would like you to continue to follow Chloe and her company of idiots. But first I need you to do something. There is a small zoo close to where you now are; I can see it from one of my shards lying about. Take this crystal with you and I will guide you to where it is." Rowena snatched it up in her mouth and walked along as Rajeem directed her through the alley ways.

Eventually she arrived at the zoo and went in.

"Now go to the eagle exhibit, it is straight ahead on this path." She made her way along the path and stopped in front of the cage. Inside of it there was a very large, proud looking eagle sitting upon a branch and looking down curiously at her. Rajeem then continued to instruct her;

"OK, now set me down next to that sign in front of you." She set the crystal down next to the plaque which hung by a brass chain and watched as a small mist emanated from it which enveloped both the sign and the crystal. When it dispersed, she saw that the plaque was now lying on the ground...next to the brass chain that it previously held, which was now fashioned as a necklace for the crystal. Rajeem further instructed;

"Now take me into the cage... but be on your guard. That bird will most likely attack you. But that is what we want. You must try to get me around his neck." Rowena answered nervously;

"Uh...ok." She picked the necklace up in her mouth and crept to the edge of the cage. She then squeezed herself between the bars of the door while looking up at the bird. Clearly the eagle looked angry and agitated with her company. She was sure it could smell her fear. It then suddenly jumped off of its perch with a screech and dove straight for her.

Rowena held her ground as it swooped down with open talons to grab her. She could tell that she had surprised it when she leaped upwards in engagement. Certainly it was only accustomed to prey which always fled in terror. This was the only thing which saved her and allowed her to succeed...the element of surprise.

Before she knew it, the chain was hanging around its neck and she was jumping off of its back and to the ground. The eagle was clearly confused and disoriented. It flew back to the safety of its perch to take stock of what had just happened.

At first it shook its head…trying to dislodge the necklace, but then suddenly it stopped. Rowena watched in remembrance as she saw in its face a different kind of consciousness awaken. It then looked her in the eye. She wasn't sure how long it would be before it could speak, but she thought that probably he could now understand what was said to him. She said to it;

"Hello Mr. Eagle, my name is Rowena. I know this is confusing for you right now… but you have just acquired the ability to understand speech, and shortly you may also be able to speak as well." She could tell that he understood her as she watched his face.

She continued; "Hmmm…I think you need a name…let me see…if you don't mind my giving it to you, how about… Pierpont?" He looked down at her with comical annoyance while shaking his head in disagreement. She was toying with him.

"Ha ha, how about….Fluffy?!" he then looked more disgusted than before as he rolled his eyes and put his wings on his hips.

"Ok, I'm just teasing you…let me see, something noble then …how about…Ethan?" He momentarily cocked his eyes in thought, then looked at her as he stuck out his chest and nodded his agreement. "Ok then…Ethan it is. Welcome to our little family. You and I are now siblings, and we also have a common purpose as well. You see…we both also have a master. He is the one responsible for the gift of our enhanced consciousness. And we also have a task at hand which needs to be fulfilled."

"We must both leave this cage and go on a journey to find our masters enemies who are currently en route to him and stop them." Ethan jumped off of his perch and landed next to her on the ground. Rowena again noticed her master's eye was visible in the crystal. It then looked up towards the cage door and commanded;

"Ethan, climb up the bars on that door to where the lock is and hold me near it." Ethan complied, and as Rowena watched she saw a bolt of energy shoot from the crystal into the lock. Ethan squawked and jumped off of the door and back to the floor. Rowena supposed he must have gotten a shock.

They both looked up at the lock and saw that it now was very much damaged and smoldering. She pushed the door and it effortlessly swung wide open.

"Well, it looks as if you are now free my brother, I bet you can't wait to spread your wings after being cooped up in this cage for who knows how long." Ethan eagerly ejected himself from the cage and flew up over the nearby trees. Rowena thought that he made quite a majestic sight as he circled above, his wingspan was surprisingly large. Just then some zoo attendants came running towards the cage. She decided it was time for her to get out of there as well, so she ran out and back down the path. As she exited the zoo, she looked up to see if Ethan was still visible above. She saw that he was following her, so she led him to someplace where they could be alone.

After a short search she found an empty courtyard that had a large fountain at its center. She went and sat next to it and waited as Ethan landed next to her on the ground.

"How was that…are you feeling better after stretching your wings?" He enthusiastically nodded in agreement.

"Well then, I suppose it is time for us to be going… I'm not sure, but I think our master intends that I must accompany you into the air. Are you game for me to climb onto your back to see if we can manage it?" Ethan nodded somewhat doubtfully, then turned to the side to allow her on. She hopped onto his back and sat while holding onto the necklace with her front paws.

"Well, it's now or never," she said. Ethan gaged her weight. He decided he would need a running start. She held on as he did and the next thing she knew they were climbing above the fountain.

She saw a small boy and girl watching and pointing at them through a window as they passed, shouting;

"Mommy, daddy… look!" the parents gasped in astonishment at the sight of a cat riding an eagle past their window. Rowena grimaced, spat a raspberry, and called out; "mind your own business you snotty nosed brats!" as they flew off.

Back at the park, Chloe and company had finished their coffee. Monty, Mr. Oppum and Chloe were making ready to continue their journey while Onri and his parents were saying their goodbyes. During their coffee break Onri's parents had agreed to his desire to continue helping the cause. When shortly they were again ready to leave, they all took their seats. Onris parents waved goodbye as they watched them rise into the air and grow smaller while miraculously floating away.

Onri couldn't help but shed a tear as he watched, and continually waved to them as they also shrank into the distance. He said;

"Oh Chloe, Monty, Mr. Oppum, and Mr. Magic Carpet…thank you all so much. I am so happy to have my parents back to me. And I want to continue making them proud of me…we must succeed in this endeavor and come home safely as well."

"I agree," Chloe replied and continued; "earlier we had talked about devising some kind of a plan... but we found that we just didn't yet know enough to be able to do so. I'm still not certain that anything has changed...let's go over what we know about Rajeems capabilities." Mr. Oppum said; "yes... yes that is a most wise idea Chloe!"

Onri stroked his chin and said;

"Let's see...primarily he is in possession of the jewel that gives him certain powers...of which we may not yet know how many." Chloe added;

"Yes... and the powers that we do know of so far are... One; he can make inanimate objects, as well as animals conscious and obey him...Two; he can create mists which can swallow and trap people...Three; that he can see from his mists and project destructive energy from them as well, and Four; he has had accomplices helping him." Mr. Oppum added;

"Well, I'm sure this is an obvious thought... separating him from the jewel worked before... but unfortunately this time he would be expecting us to try that...and he is waiting for us, so there is no element of surprise." Chloe agreed;

"Yes, having no element of surprise is a primary dilemma. So, ultimately we need to again separate him from the jewel either by having it covertly taken, or by us confronting him directly and taking it." Onri added;

"And also I wouldn't object to the idea of destroying him bodily if it came to that...and we felt capable of it!" Monty joined in;

"Well those are our objectives... we just need some kind of plan..." Mr. Carpet said;

"If I may make a suggestion, let us journey in silence for a while, hopefully to help clear our minds and see if we can come up with something that is out of the box...something that would not be easily predicted by him." They all agreed, and for a good length of time they relaxed in thought as they enjoyed watching the French countryside below transition into the sun drenched and sun flowered fields of Italy.

Guided by their master, Rowena and Ethan flew in double time to try and catch up to their prey. After a few hours Rajeem asked; "Ethan, you have superior bird sight...do you see that pinpoint up ahead on the horizon?"

"Yes my master."

"That is them... you must come upon them as suddenly as possible before they get a chance to notice you. It could work if you were able to fly faster. If not, we would need to trail them for a while and wait to ambush them after they have landed someplace." Ethan answered; "It is possible for me to fly significantly faster for a short time...I think I can do it." Rowena was surprised when their speed doubled, and meowed as she gripped the necklace more tightly.

Chloe and company had a short time ago passed the mainland of Italy and were now above the jeweled waters of the Mediterranean. Onri pointed ahead, saying;

"We are coming upon the isle of Sicily, it may be time for us to land and rest a bit...maybe have some supper and camp for the night." Monty perked up;

"That sounds like a good plan, my little bones are getting weary and in need of some walking upon land." Just as he finished speaking he felt a painful grip on his shoulders, and before he knew what had happened he was horrified to find that he was gripped in the talons of a large bird of prey...which was any mouse's most primal fear!

"Help...Help...Chloe... Onri help me!" he screamed, as he looked back at them. Onri shouted;

"Look... it's that cat from before, and it's riding atop that eagle... I can't believe it!" Chloe answered;

"I can... and we need to act fast to save him!" Before they could react, Ethan circled around and headed straight for them. It was then that Chloe noticed the necklace... and the familiar emanating mist which quickly expanded and revealed the enlarged eye. Chloe reached behind her into the tent and grabbed her staff, as Onri also grabbed his sword. The eye crackled with energy, as did Chloe's staff.

As both parties sped towards one another they were preceded by fantastical bursts of energy which violently crashed together in flashes of intense light and ear splitting cracks. Both parties were very close together when this happened and none escaped the perilous effects. Screams of pain and surprise could be heard coming from them all as they collided in midair amid a cloud of smoke, sparks, feathers, and falling debris.

They and the whole mess fell and splashed into the sea. Chloe and Onri quickly regained their senses while choking and coughing up salty water. Chloe then saw Mr. Carpet floating nearby upon the surface. A significant corner of him was burned away. The chest was intact and floating nearby next to an unconscious and sinking Mr. Oppum. Onri, still clutching his sword, tossed it onto Mr. Carpet and swam over to help Mr. Oppum. When he got there he placed him upon the chest and towed it towards Mr. Carpet, then hauled it and himself onboard.

Chloe, also still clutching her staff, looked around and was surprised to see a very singed and frightened looking Monty swimming towards her. She plucked him onto her back and swam over to Mr. Carpet and climbed aboard as well and said;

"I can't believe it… we're all still of this earth!
…though I'm terribly afraid for Mr. Oppum!"

"… I see no sign of our attackers… maybe they perished
and sank!" offered Monty. Onri then asked;
"Mr. Carpet, are you okay… can you still fly?"
"Yes, I think so."

"Then quickly if you can, we need to get to land and attend to Mr. Oppum." They then rose just above the surface of the sea and traveled the short distance to the island.

Once upon the sand, Chloe and Onri more closely examined poor Mr. Oppum. Chloe reported;

"I checked that he was breathing out there on the water, and I see now that it is still so...Mr. Oppum...can you hear me...Mr. Oppum...? "Onri said;

"I suppose we can be quite thankful that he is alive, but for the time being I think that all we can do is make him comfortable and hope he regains consciousness."

"Yes...let's move into the shade and shelter of that palm grove over there," Chloe pointed. Once they were there, Onri proposed; "This tent is in tatters, but I think that it's all still here, let us see if we can re-erect it." They all then set about the task. It had a few holes burnt into it, but it was still usable. Chloe placed the blankets and pillows onto a rock out in the sun to dry...then decided that she would see what was salvageable inside the chest to make a meal from. Onri built a small camp fire, and soon the three of them were sitting around it and watching a pot of canned soup as it warmed.

After they finished eating, Chloe said;

"Since it looks as if we may be here for a spell, I think I need to seclude myself with this staff and see if I can bring myself to understand and control some of its powers. So far all I have been doing is instinctively reacting to events as they unfold. But to have any real hope of succeeding, I think that I will need to be able do more." Mr. Carpet added;

"Yes, that is quite logical. Also I have been thinking about our strategy going forward and I came up with one possible idea. Since we have thought that we needed to come up with something unexpected, maybe we should just do the opposite of what the expected course would be." He continued;

"At this point, Rajeem is probably expecting that we will continue to come straight to him…to challenge him directly. But that I think is not a good plan. He would be on his own turf, in full control of all of his powers, and he would probably have an army of support. We could not hope to prevail under such circumstances. No, I think we need to draw him out of his protections… catch him off guard somehow…somewhere." Onri offered;

"That is brilliant, yes… after Mr. Oppum hopefully recovers, and Chloe has more mastery over her powers…maybe we should journey closer to him…but not too close. But just far enough away for him to feel he was still near the safety of his home."

"Yes, I think that is exactly the right idea," Chloe said as she grasped her staff, which was lying next to her, and continued; "Good thinking! Well, I think I will go find a retreat some place nearby and study this jewel for a time, hopefully I will learn something more of its powers."

"Good luck," they chimed in unison.

Chloe wandered a short distance away and found a comfortable spot to sit in the shade next to a palm tree where there was a view of the beach and sea. She sat upon the sand, resting her back against a palm tree, and stared wistfully out at the sea. She listened to the ebb and flow of the tide. It lulled her into a peaceful state of mind which felt very cleansing.

After a spell of daydreaming, she remembered what she had come here for and picked up her staff which was lying next to her. She rested the jeweled head of it lightly against her temple, and continued to stare out to sea and let her mind wander where it may. Then slowly, she hadn't realized when, her thoughts began to feel like they were aligning with some sort of an entity…a sort of presence. It felt so natural and comfortingly familiar, like a mothers love. She eagerly let herself be swallowed up by this feeling…almost afraid it would disappear if she focused too intently upon it. But it didn't fade…it gently intensified into a kind of tangible rapture.

She began to feel that her mind and body were merging with the earth… and that, as she was always a part of it before…she now felt a part of its collective consciousness. Somehow she felt that it spoke to her…but without speaking. It was revealing its secrets to her. She closed her eyes. Colors and scents of the earth pervaded her thoughts…the musty browns of soil, the beiges and grays of rocks, the fresh and salty blues and greens of water.

With a feeling of complete ecstasy, she mentally surrendered all of her minds' defenses…and immediately upon doing so, she felt her consciousness explode outwards. It sank deep into the earth…seemingly melding with all matter as it travelled…the soil, the vegetation and its' roots, the water, the living bacteria, the insects, the animals above and below the surface…then, when she felt that she had reached the conductive elements of the oceans and seas, the velocity of her propagation reached nearly the speed of light.

She heard herself catch her breath as she almost instantaneously encircled the globe. She could see the colored rainbows of all the fishes of the seas. Her velocity halted as she felt the journey of envelopment complete. She seethed...pulsated...she felt the outer limits of the earths' atmosphere confining her expansion. The earthly elements of life beckoned the inclusion and reunion with star matter, it was just beyond her reach, but calling to her... she reached out...and felt that it was possible to close the distance to the next body of matter. Then, like a frightened child she pulled her figurative hand back...the cold dark vacuum of space was too terrifying.

Her thoughts returned to her earthly envelopment. Elemental knowledge flooded her being. Her eyes were still closed back at that pinpoint of a location where her body still sat with the jeweled staff resting upon her temple, she could see herself sitting there...and at the same time she could see outwards from that position as well. She linked the elements of the jewel to like kinds below her.

A multi-paralleled phosphorous web established itself and held fast in a circuit of electron flow. She willed part of her consciousness to emanate from the top of the staff, and felt it flow outwards within an amethyst mist. She found she could also see outwards from this as well. She expanded this medium and looked back to see herself still sitting there motionless. She didn't know how, but knew that physical travel could be possible within it...and advanced it towards and enveloped her own body. She then willed the mist to arise and float towards her companions at their camp.

Monty and Onri were engaged in conversation with Mr. Carpet on how to best revive their friend Mr. Oppum when they were startled and alarmed at the arrival of the mist. Monty jumped up from where he was sitting and pointed;

"Look, quickly....run for cover!" and dove into the brush. Onri stood and unsheathed his sword, shouting;

"Stay back...!" as he brandished a defensive position. The mist then touched down in front of him, consolidated...then quickly dissipated. As the purple wisps cleared, there stood Chloe; one hand on her hip, the other upon her staff. Wide eyed disbelief and slackened jaws greeted her.

"Chloe...how...look at your eyes, your hair...and your finger nails! They've changed color!" remarked Onri. She looked at her hands, and sure enough her finger nails were now a light shade of violet.

"Oh my...well I'm glad that I do like the color," she laughed. Onri said;

"And your hair is still red, but it now has...iridescent purple highlights...it's beautiful!" Chloe giggled with delight,

"Really?"

"And your eyes are still blue, but they're also tinted with that same color...what happened...how did you do all of this?" She answered;

"I was sitting with my staff and the next thing that I knew...it felt like my mind became one with the earth. I could see everything inside of it...and how the jewel is related to it."

"Well, obviously you have succeeded in doing what you had set out to do."

"Yes, I do feel that I now know much more about the jewel...and very relieved that we may now have a fighting chance."

She looked over at poor Mr. Oppum; he was still lying there motionless next to the tent. She walked over and knelt next to him. Placing her palm to his forehead, she closed her eyes and tried to see if there was now anything she could do to help him. She could see a misalignment in his brain to his body...she nudged it slightly with her mind and pulled away her hand. She opened her eyes and watched his face for a moment.

"Mr. Oppum...can you hear me?" He opened his eyes, sat up and looked at them all, saying;

"Oh my...have I over slept again?" They all laughed.

"Oh wait...now I remember, is everyone alright?"

"Yes, now we are. How do you feel?" asked Onri.

"I think I'm feeling fine," he said, as he stood and walked in a circle. He stopped and held out his arms.

"See?"

"Yay!" they all cheered and applauded.

Chapter 9

Rowena and Ethan found themselves inside the mist immediately after the impact. Most of Ethan's feathers were now either missing or singed off, making flight impossible. Their master's eye looked down at them.

"Our first attempt to destroy our enemy has failed. I am now transporting you to another location where you can rest and recuperate; you will remain there until I have more instructions for you." With that said, the mist evaporated and they found themselves in some unknown woods.

"Well, this is just great, it looks like we will be stuck here for a long time," lamented Rowena.

Back at the camp, Chloe was rummaging through their chest of provisions while saying;

"It seems we're running very low on food here, we will need to replenish our supplies." Onri offered;

"You and I should go and see what we can find. Mr. Oppum … Monty, would you mind staying here and watching over things?"

"It would be our pleasure, but please be careful," replied Mr. Oppum. Chloe and Onri then set off inland towards where they imagined they would find a village or a town. After a short distance of walking through the sand, they came to a small steep hill which they clambered up. Once at the top they saw that they were at the edge of a very large, old, and bustling city. Onri said;

"I believe we are in the Italian…or Sicilian city of Palermo, and not far from here we should find a large outdoor market that I have heard about."

They traversed a few blocks of antiquated apartment buildings; then came upon a wide street of chaotic traffic to their left. A traffic attendant was standing in the midst of a melee of autos, trucks, and Vespa's. They whirred to and fro as he waved his arms and blew his whistle in a seemingly vain attempt at directing them. Chloe noticed a large train station beyond him on the far side of the intersection. She also couldn't help but notice the dazzling reflections of light coming from many jeweled statues assembled in that far court yard. A chill suddenly went through her heart as she realized what they indeed were….

"Onri, look over there at all of those statues!"

"Yes I see them"

"We must go over to them." They made their way along with the throngs of people crossing the boulevard, passing the traffic attendant along the way. Once there, Chloe did a quick head count. "More than one hundred souls here are all petrified… this is horrific…ghastly!" Chloe made her way into the midst of them. Once she felt that she was out of view, she held out her staff. With her free hand she placed her palm over her closed eyelids. She again felt her consciousness flow outwards as before.

She could see that they were all still alive, but in some kind of stasis... their thoughts were also frozen in terror... just like the expressions upon their faces. She willed them to be unfrozen. Phosphorus plasma emanated from the elements of like crystals far beneath her feet which directed to the base of her staff. She then smartly tapped it to the ground.

Onri was still standing on the fringe of the crystalline crowd when he saw the bright flash of violet light. A halo of energy also quickly expanded outwards which passed through and beyond him, tickling his skin and pricking his hair as it went. He turned his head and watched the halo travel through and past all of the surprised people and the buildings as it went.

He looked back at the crowd in front of him. The jeweled surfaces of them began to turn more opaque. And he watched as the color of life began to return to all of their faces. Within only a few seconds they were all standing there and looking around. Looks of realization spread between them as they saw that they were all again free. They cheered and hugged one another.

Onri heard a simultaneous honking of many car horns. The traffic had stopped and people were rushing out of their cars to make their way over to revel with them in their freedom. The scene became very chaotic. Chloe made her way out of the crowd as the people thanked and groped at her with teary eyes and kind words. They noticed that the roar of car horns and cheers were not limited to the immediate vicinity. Onri speculated;

"There must have been many more captives throughout the city which were also just revived... this is just deafening!" People were jostling to take pictures and videos of them with their smart phones. Chloe said;

"Oh my, it looks as though we will be in the media once again. I'm afraid that everyone I know is now aware of where I am and what I'm doing. Well, at least they won't be afraid of not knowing what has become of me." Onri added;

"Let us try to get away from here quickly without being followed... I think I know which way that market is, as it has been described to me before."

They then darted under the legs of some of the adults before them and made their way back across the wide street of gridlocked traffic and cheering people. Chloe again felt incognito after traveling just a short distance through the crowd, as no one now seemed aware of them. She followed Onri as he made his way down another main boulevard which was perpendicular from the one they had just left.

The going was somewhat slowed by the gathering crowds. After just a couple of blocks they turned left and crossed this street and proceeded down one of the narrow alleyways. Very tall, old apartment buildings lined either side of them, stung across with many cords of drying laundry. They snaked along the dimly lit winding cobblestones for an extended jaunt, and then suddenly came out into a bright and open pedestrian thoroughfare.

The scene was also very chaotic here as well, if not more so. This was definitely the city market place that they were searching for. Both sides of the lane were lined with carts and store fronts, chock full of produce and anything else one would need as far as food was concerned. Chloe still had some money left, but when she tried to approach any of the vendors to inquire or buy anything, she found that all business had halted in the excitement, so much so that many of the carts were being accidentally overturned by the jubilance of the celebratory crowd. Onri offered;

"Well, I think we've earned to just take what we need, we have to get out of here and back to the camp." They scooped up provisions here and there as they quickly made their way along the lane. They came upon the next alley way which would again take them back towards whence they came. After darting through it, they again made their way back to the edge of town to the beach. The going was slow, as the crowds had greatly thickened.

When they finally made it back to their camp, they collapsed onto Mr. Carpet, dropping all of their supplies along with them, and giggling uncontrolledly. Chloe said, followed by Onri;

"Ha ha, I'm so exhausted."

"I am too." Mr. Oppum and Monty stood there looking at them with their hands on their hips, watching as Chloe and Onri rolled around laughing among the chocolate bars, bananas, and many wrapped slices of pepperoni pizza. Monty and Mr. Oppum looked at each other confusedly... looked back at the silly infectious scene, and then decided to jump into the party. They all laughed and ate the goodies to their hearts content.

It was getting late in the evening by the time they had finished eating while Chloe and Onri had relayed the recent events. They all decided to retire for a good night's sleep, and in the morning they would make their plans for going forward.

While Chloe slept, she had a dream. She and her compatriots were again traveling upon Mr. Carpet, but this time they were not in the sky, but under the sea. It seemed somewhat dark as they sped along the ocean floor. The main source of light was emanating from her staff. She somehow felt that there was a purpose for them being down there...as it seemed she was in contact with the earth spirit once again. She also had this weird feeling that she was in immediate danger.

Suddenly she was awakened by some trauma that was happening in the camp. It took a few moments to clear the sleepy cobwebs of sleep. But when she was fully awake it now seemed a nightmare. Their camp was flooded with a risen tide. But the water was not acting in a normal fashion. It was roiling around to and fro, as if trying to drown them all. Onri was attempting to shimmy up a palm tree while screaming to her to wake up. Mr. Carpet was submerged, and the tent had washed away. She saw that Mr. Oppum and Monty were both clutching at the bum of Onri's pants. The sky was blotted out with thick storm clouds which seemed in the dark to be of a purple hue.

Thunder and violet lightning was booming and cracking frenetically, and each time it did, it seemed the whole scene in front of her polarized in a negative photographic effect. Chloe had not yet been able to grab onto anything to save herself as she clutched her staff in the turbulence. She felt that her legs were being held onto by something.

As the lightning flashed again, she saw a mouth form in the waves around her, and it was attempting to devour her! Instinctively, she knew that it would be her death to let it do so, as she was already out of breath and choking on the salty water. She raised her staff out of the water and above her head as, impossibly, coconuts from the trees above began simultaneously pelting her from all directions. She almost felt her consciousness lapsing from the painful onslaught.

She needed to immediately take control of this situation or she was done for. She willed the jeweled mist to emanate from her staff and encapsulate them all. In the flash of an instant, they were all lying together in a soggy mess upon Mr. Carpet inside the safe and silent cocoon.

They untangled themselves and sat there for a good while to catch their breath, as they looked amongst each other and their surroundings.

Chloe saw that her earlier dream was now a reality, as they were now under water and thankfully enveloped in a life sustaining violet colored bubble. Chloe asked;

"Is everyone alright?" Onri replied;

"Oh my goodness, thank you for the quick thinking, we were all almost done for. I was sleeping, then all of a sudden…all hell broke loose." Monty then asked;

"But…where are we?" Mr. Oppum answered him;

"I do believe we are now under the sea, which moments ago seemed intent upon our demise." Chloe then offered;

"I think it will be possible for us to travel along the sea floor for a time. Maybe it will benefit us to stay out of sight, and let Rajeem think he has succeeded in drowning us all. Mr. Carpet, are you also alright?"

"Yes I am fine, I don't require air to breath, so I was never in immediate danger."

"Okay, that is a relief. Now we only need to relax while I direct our movements down here."

"I will also see if I can affect our drying out of this soggy state as we go." Chloe moved to the front of them and sat cross legged as she held out her staff to light the way. They were soon gliding along the sandy floor, traversing deeper and deeper as they went. They watched as the sand became interspersed with rocks, and then boulders. They were certainly in another world of sorts as they traveled along the bottom of the sea.

It was beautiful. They passed over immense white coral reefs with whole populations of colored fishes going about their business. Onri marveled as they passed an old Spanish ship wreck. He wished he could go exploring for sunken treasure. They all kept busy with wondrous curiosity, and hadn't noticed that they were now indeed dry and quite comfortable.

Chloe sat as if in a trance, she felt the entity of her dream. It pervaded her being, and she once again felt a oneness with it and the entire planet...that soothing rhythmic pulsing of finiteness. It was guiding her thoughts as well as their direction. She felt the age of the earth. Or more directly, the age of all of the living matter upon and inside of it.

She could see the ancient paths that time and evolution had taken from the beginning to the present. Here on the floor of the sea, it was the completely relevant place to view this saga, as all life on the planet began in these waters. She could see the genetic memories of the volcanic flows that oozed the star stuff of life... proteins evolving into multi celled creatures.

As the eons passed, life dragged itself out of the oceans and onto dry land. The age of the reptiles and dinosaurs came, and then was destroyed by the very same hands of outer space which had helped create it in the first place, when it had thrown at the earth a mountain sized asteroid. More time passed as she saw life on the surface reinvent itself after the atmosphere recovered. Then she was aware of the time of man. It was a relatively short time from the beginnings of it until now...but in that time she could see a significant degradation of the health of the planets' living matter. All life on the planet was now on a speeding path of degeneration. She could see the cellular memories of the multitudes of extinct species which were now forever lost from the forests, and down here from the oceans as well.

She had been feeling that their direction of travel was somehow being guided along. And now it seemed that they had arrived someplace. In the path of where they were advancing was the yawning black mouth of an immense cave. They all noticed it at the same moment. Mr. Oppum queried;

"Oh my...we're not going into that nasty looking hole are we?" Chloe answered him;

"It appears that I am being guided there, but all is well and I am completely sure that we will be perfectly safe in there." Onri added; "Well, if you're sure, then that is good enough for me." They entered the complete blackness of the cave. All except Chloe looked behind them to watch the wonders of the oceanic world recede. In only a few moments they were in complete blackness, which was very disorienting. Their only light from Chloe's staff seemed wholly inefficient in illuminating anything, as even the walls of the cave were lost to them. Chloe closed her eyes.

The unspoken voice in her mind was very concise in its directions and she gave herself to them completely. Their direction seemed to now be angled almost completely in a downward direction, and for the space of more than two hours that is the path they took...straight down towards the center of the earth.

Finally, after what seemed like forever, they felt their direction of movement level off and progress in a forward motion. Almost immediately they were all startled to see something other than blackness... the protuberance of a rocky ceiling very close to their heads. Onri said;

"It looks like we may be close to the end of our journey...I see some light up ahead." They passed the end of the cave's ceiling, and it was replaced by what clearly looked like the surface of the water...with light above it. They then surfaced and traveled a little further to the edge of a black sandy shore. Mr. Carpet took them onto the dry beach and stopped.

The spectacle that greeted them was awe inspiring to say the least. They all stood stupefied...and mesmerized as they stared off into the impossible distance of what was clearly a rain forest. But they were not outside on the surface. The sky, if you wanted to call it that, was all a light mist. There was a light source off in the distance, which most certainly was an active volcano...with a trail of magma flowing downwards from it.

There were mountains covered with dense trees, which were all draped in vines. And every inch of the grounds beyond the beach were covered with green ferns. And the flowers...there were many different kinds and colors everywhere one looked... mostly growing off of the vines. The air was humidly warm and florally fragrant. It was intoxicating just to breathe it in. They all looked at one another. Chloe said;

"I can't believe this is real, I want to pinch myself to see if I'm dreaming." She closed her eyes and pinched her forearm. When she opened her eyes, she was still standing there with her wonderful friends in this glorious place, which caused her to excitedly embrace them while jumping up and down.

"Oh, my lovely friends...isn't this a beautiful place!?" They all joined in the infectious group hug, exclaiming;

"Yay!" Onri then spied something a short distance away and pointed;

"Look, just through the ferns there...I see banana, guava, mango, and papaya trees all laden with fruit just waiting to be eaten!" Mr. Oppum and Monty exclaimed;

"Yum...let's go!" Chloe said;

"You all go ahead; I feel there is something I need to do just now. I'll see you in a little while... just save me some fruit...ha ha!"

Chloe watched them trip over themselves laughing as they dashed through the ferns. She now felt herself being called in the opposite direction of her friends into the forest. She turned and walked slowly, taking in the wondrous sights and smells, stopping here and there to smell a flower...to touch a fuzzy plant. Without noticing when, the calling in her mind had stopped. She looked around her to see if anything looked amiss or out of place. Without noticing anything out of the ordinary for this very inordinate place, she sat down on a brownish sort of rock that was next to her and decided to wait until hopefully she felt something again.

"...Hello Chloe." She alarmingly stood up...looking around her. There was no one around, and she began to wonder if her mind had only played a trick on her. She chanced;

"Hello...is someone there?"

"Yes I am here...but I hope that my appearance won't frighten you," the voice said again. It seemed to come from the rock where she had just been sitting. She looked closer at it...why, it wasn't a rock at all. It was a... just then a head popped out of a large hole at one end of it... and legs did as well from other orifices.

"Oh my, you're a sea tortoise? I'm sorry that I sat on you...I thought you were a rock."

"Yes, I am in the form of a tortoise right now...but only for the purpose of speaking with you. Actually I have never before taken the form of a living creature during my whole existence, as I have never had the need to speak with a human. It is nice to make your acquaintance Chloe; you can call me...if I may be so bold...Mother." Chloe answered;

"It is finally nice to meet you Mother." Mother continued;

"I know from your memories that you recently lost your own parents…I hope that your calling me this will not be distressing for you. If it is, you may call me anything that you like."

"No, I feel Mother is the perfect name for you." Mother went on; "There is much to discuss…to start with…the staff that you're holding which contains the 'life jewel'. That jewel contains the element which bestows consciousness. It is not normally in a form which is accessible anyone."

"But I recently made it so and placed it in the path of a human to find it so that I may become in communication with your race. Also through it one is able to channel the elemental energies of this planet. I know that while on your way here you have seen played before your mind the histories of all life on this world. Those histories are readily accessible due to the natural order of life and its' evolutional memories. And no doubt you have seen the rapid degeneration of all life since the evolution of human kind has brought him to the forefront of planet wide domination."

"The other human who has possession of this jewel has continually ignored my summons and has also been using its bestowed powers for his own selfish gains…as well as wreaking more havoc to life on the planet. My existence is nothing more than a collective consciousness. I am an amalgam of all awareness. All life on the planet has consciousness on its own plane of existence and communicates with its peers."

"Since the beginnings of life on this planet, there has never before been a species that had the power to affect to such a large degree, the health and ultimate fate of all life and consciousness across all of the planes. It is the evolution of the human brain which gives them the ability to harness and control the earths' elements. This is not a bad thing; it is the completely logical and natural course for him. But evolution is a continuum, and while all of the other species have always lived by consuming only what they needed to survive, man has evolved to obsessively consume far more than what is needed. The energy used and the pollution which is created in this process is threatening the extinction of all of us."

There was a pause in mothers' speech. Chloe thought maybe it was intended for her to ask questions, so she queried;

"Yes, I see that now…and I am sorry. I do apologize for my whole species. But is there anything that I can do to help?" Mother continued;

"Apology accepted…yes, that is why I have called you here. The changes that need to be done require a human emissary, for the havoc that will ensue for your kind will be significant and probably cause death and hardship for many of you. In good conscience I could not make these changes without permission from one of you." Chloe offered;

"Oh my…this makes me feel very afraid… and unworthy of any kind of decision to be made for the whole of us…"

Mother continued; "That is understandable, but if nothing is done, the consequences would be far worse and possibly result in your own extinction... as well as to most other planetary life. Unfortunately, it most probably is already too late. The planets' atmosphere, through the burning of fossil fuels, has already deteriorated to a point that a resulting ice age is rapidly approaching. The oceans will rise and greatly reduce the amount of dry land for all species involved, to survive upon it. Humans would probably survive through this period by burrowing and living mostly underground. But they would still continue burning fossil fuels, and also using, to a more devastating effect, nuclear fission power generation."

"This is also highly poisonous for all of us and must cease to be done as well." Chloe asked; "What do you propose... is there anything that can be done?"

"I think that humans would have eventually learned to balance their consumption with the necessity of preserving their own lives and that of the entire planet, but the time for it has run out. A drastic change is needed now. I propose an action which I can easily cause to affect."

"By slightly altering the elemental composition of the worlds' fossil fuel that is currently underground, I can cause it to become noncombustible and useless. Also I can make another type of elemental change to uranium which will render it into a different form and also unusable as well." Chloe offered;

"If you could do that, it sounds like it would be a pretty painless remedy." Mother replied;

"Yes, it sounds like an easy solution. It would at least halt the continuing destruction. But we would still need to survive the unavoidable advancing environmental devastation. For mankind, these challenges will indeed be monumental. For the changes I make will also cause him immediate catastrophic social trauma. The entire economic structure that is your current global model will completely collapse as the basis of monetary valuation loses its' foundation…energy."

"Suddenly, there will be no mass transit or convenient travel to anyplace, and the current systems of food distribution to centers of population will also cease to be, for there will no longer be combustion engines for these purposes."

"And your whole business model will also have to be transformed, as the employment that most people hold will cease to exist in its current form. Also, the mental health of the entire community of man will suffer a massive and unrelenting psychotic episode, as starvation and fear of the unknown will cause riots, violence, and suicide."

"Man will suddenly need to start living in very small communities that are self-sustaining. It would be a great help to your kind if there was someone to explain what is happening and what could be a way forward, for I think it would save a great many lives. It could be dangerous for you though, to be put in a position of that kind of perceived power. Many will wrongly think that you caused this to happen."

"So I offer to you and your loved ones the hospitality of this place to live during these times, to keep you safe and to continue to be the human emissary. You and your future descendants will need to continue this work for them, explaining and exacting more necessary changes as time goes on. And you will need the continued power of the jewel to do this work, so it is necessary that I keep it active and in existence."

"But the other human who has possession of it has no need for it…and it must to be taken from him, for he would use it to undermine the very work that we would be doing."

Chloe was feeling a little overwhelmed by all of this information. The sheer gravity of the coming situation for the worlds' populations was mind boggling. She sat down on the black lava-like sand and rested her back against the trunk of a large fern. Mother was now silent after her diatribe, and was munching on some nearby foliage.

Chloe closed her eyes for a time to rest her mind and let it all sink in… she felt sad and couldn't help but cry. She dreaded the thought of the responsibility of having to relay this catastrophic information to the world, and thought that she would feel…a lack of authority. Well, by the time that her part in this was over…of separating Rajeem from the jewel…she would surely by then be a more recognized figure through all of the continued media coverage. As uncomfortable as this thought was for her, she would have to take more advantage of being in the spotlight in the near future.

Chloe hadn't noticed that she had fallen into a deep and dreamless sleep while sitting there. As she was fully awake now, she really could not tell how long she had been sleeping there. The light never changed in this place and she thought it may have been several hours later by now. She creakily rose to her feet; her back ached from leaning on that blasted fern. She looked around her…Mother Tortoise was nowhere to be seen. 'I better go find the others; they may be worrying about me' she thought, and made her way back to where she had last seen them scampering into the forest to eat the fruit that Onri had pointed out.

Well, she certainly had found them once she got there. And by the looks of it they hadn't been worried about her in the least. She giggled out loud as she surveyed the scene of them all sleeping here and there on the black sand among their sizable piles of spent fruit rinds, peels, and pits. Mr. Oppum was of course loudly snoring as usual. "Well, I should let all of you finish sleeping." She said quietly to herself. She noticed again that she was feeling extremely happy and content to be in this beautiful place just now.

Also… was that the sound of running fresh water she heard somewhere just beyond her sleeping friends? After walking past them a short distance and peering through the foliage, there indeed was a large lake of crystal clear water. It was fed by a stream which was cascading down some rocks on the far end. She went and dipped her toe into it to test the temperature. "Oh my…it's as warm as an evening bath," she said to herself.

She wasted no time in stripping to her under garments and wading right in. She spent some considerable time floating to and fro on her back, and also lounging on this and that shore. Finally, after what had seemed a couple of hours later, she saw her friends appear over on the bank where she had at first waded in.

"Hello!" she called out while waving. Mr. Oppum and Monty immediately jumped into the water, and Onri wasn't far behind after he quickly stripped nude and dove in.

Chloe couldn't help but laugh as she watched his skinny little white and naked body dive in. Some things, she thought, were for some reason just universally funny. In no time they all were swimming around each other playing splashing games, laughing, and generally carrying on. After a good while they all got out and laid themselves down to relax on the warm black shore. Onri joined them after donning his undergarment. After a few minutes when Chloe had caught her breath, she thought that it was now a good time to fill them in on what had transpired with her and Mother. "My friends, I met someone very special earlier when we separated, and she explained all of the strange circumstances of this whole endeavor…"

When Chloe had finished her tale, they continued lying there on their backs and staring up into the misty sky. No one had uttered a word for some time, as it was a lot to take in. Onri got up, found the rest of his clothes and put them on. He said;

"Well, I guess I shouldn't be surprised to hear such an incredible explanation…when our whole tale thus far has been equally fantastic. But I worry now about my parents and what will happen to us after Mothers' new changes take effect." Chloe answered;

"I'm sure all of you would be welcome to live here with me if you thought that you would like to. We would always be able to come and go from here as we pleased…I shouldn't think that we would be trapped here for any reason." Mr. Oppum and Monty piped in;

"Really…truly we could?"

"Of course you could, we would all be one happy family here." Onri also added;

"That would be wonderful, although I am truly sad for what will happen to the world. I hope that my parents will agree to come here with me."

Chapter 10

Chloe and company had Mr. Carpet join them on the banks of the lake. They decided it was time to make a plan for moving forward. Chloe said;

"Onri, you had an idea earlier that we might find a location someplace near our adversary and wait for him to come to us... depriving him of the major advantage of strength that he would naturally have on his own turf. I think that is still a good plan." Onri countered;

"Well thank you...when do you propose that we leave?"

"I can't think of any reason to put it off, we may as well begin to get ready for our departure." Monty offered;

"Mr. Oppum and I had good success yesterday climbing the fruit trees. We will go now and pick some more for our journey." "Righto," added Mr. Oppum, as they merrily scampered off.

After a short while they were ready to leave. Chloe said;

"There is no need for me to find Mother in order to say goodbye…as she is already here with us in my mind. Let us now be off…" Once again they all made themselves comfortable on Mr. Carpet as they sat facing forward. Chloe put her staff upon her lap as she directed clear violet colored bubble of an atmosphere again enveloped them. She said;

"Ok Mr. Carpet, you know the way." They rose up off of the black sand and sailed to a moderate height. As they circled around towards the entrance, they were afforded one last look at the paradise of this place with its mountains of flowered trees, the lake, and the spectacular erupting and flaming volcano in the distance.

Then Mr. Carpet descended towards the entrance pool and they seamlessly slid beneath the surface as Chloe again let the jewels power guide them out. After enduring the two plus hour journey through the blackness, they were finally out of the cave and over the sea floor. Chloe wasted no time in travelling to the surface, and before they knew it, they were shooting out of the water and into the sky above the Mediterranean. Onri said;

"Whew, it's nice to be out in the fresh air again."

"I'll second that," said Chloe, adding;

"I think that we could only stand a couple more hours of traveling and we will need to stop for the night, where do you think that we may be by then Onri?"

"I should think that on our present course we will be passing Greece at some point." Sure enough, as two hours went by, they were flying above the many islands of the country of Greece. Most were small and unpopulated. They decided to land on one that was populated so that they could find some much needed food and supplies.

"That one coming up looks promising," Chloe said, as she pointed. It had a quaint looking village of white washed villas which all had matching navy blue trim. They looked stunning against the crystal blue waters of the sea. They landed just outside of the town on a small hill amongst a grove of olive trees.

There were some ancient Grecian ruins over on the next hill, and Chloe could see their beige columns between the trees as she stepped off of Mr. Carpet. Onri said;

"The town is just over there; shall we go and see if we can find our supper?" Chloe answered;

"Yes, lets the four of us go. I think that we need to start spending less time hiding from the public and establish our presence in the media as trying to help the worlds' situation."

The four of them walked down the hill towards the town on a small dirt road which was lined on both sides by old, low rock walls. As they rounded a bend they came upon a man and woman riding in a garishly painted cart being pulled by a donkey, which was coming towards them. The man had a pipe in his mouth, but as he noticed them, it fell onto his lap as he opened it in astonishment. His wife also stared in disbelief. Both parties stared and watched the other as they passed. Onri said;

"Do you think they recognized us, or are they just bewildered to see such an odd party of strangers walking by?" Chloe laughed;

"Ha ha, I guess we will never know!"

Once they got to the town, they walked down the main street upon the sidewalk. The town was right along the beach and the sparkling sea was in plain view. There were many pedestrians going about their business, walking in and out of the stores or standing and talking at the outdoor vegetable stands.

Chloe saw that as more and more people noticed them walking along, they stopped what they were doing and became quiet while looking at them. Onri said;

"Let's stop at this outdoor market and see if we can find our provisions." They walked into the little lane of carts which all had awnings for shade, and stopped at one that had bread, cured meats, cheese, and fruit for sale. Attending the stand was a man, his wife, and their small son. Chloe said to Onri;

"We don't have much money left, not even enough to feed us all tonight." The man looked at his wife, and then back at them and said;

"Excuse me, but I'm sure that we recognize you from the news reports on television. The media has been trying to piece together your travels...and accomplishments. The few pictures and videos that exist of you are played continuously. What are your names?"

"I'm Chloe, and this is Onri; my friend from France."

"And these two are Monty and Mr. Oppum," Chloe said, as she indicated her little friends on the ground. The family seemed truly mesmerized as they peered over the table at Monty and Mr. Oppum, who said in unison;

"Hello." The three family members were visibly taken aback by their speech and looked at one another. They momentarily spoke amongst themselves in their native language, and then looked back at them.

"We're very happy to meet you," the man said. He introduced himself and his family;

"I'm Antoni, this is my wife Erika, and my son Nicola. I heard you say that you were low on money. Don't worry...you won't need any of that with us. We'll gladly supply you with what you need."

"Thank you, that is very kind," replied Chloe. She then noticed that a crowd was forming around them, and some of them were recording video of it with their personal devices. Erika then asked;

"Is it really true that you are working to help free the world from the grip of that mad man from India?" Chloe answered her, and spoke to the crowd as well.

"Yes it is true." She then spoke quietly into Onri's ear;

"I think you better quickly gather our supplies…" The next question came from a man right in front of her who was also recording video of them;

"Chloe, was that an actual video of you flying on a magic carpet among the skyscrapers of New York City? Many people are saying that it wasn't real." She answered;

"Yes, it was us and it was real." Someone else then asked;

"But how are you doing this…are you fighting Rajeem, and flying on carpets using…magic?" Chloe again answered;

"It may seem like magic, but it is not. There is an elemental science that has been revealed to me by a protector of the earth. It is the same science that Rajeem is using against the wishes of that same entity." She saw that the crowd was getting quite large, and it was starting to spook her. She didn't want to be afraid for their safety.

Onri looked at her and intimated that he had a full bag of supplies and was ready to leave. She continued speaking;

"I am happy to answer your questions and will be doing so again in the near future. But right now we have some pressing matters to attend to and must leave. I ask that, please, no one follow as we leave town just now…thank you." With that, she scooped Monty and Mr. Oppum up off the ground and put them upon either of her shoulders. Onri parted the crowd for them, and they proceeded through it as the many well-wishers cheered for them. They heard more questions directed to them as they passed;

"Where are your parents?"

"Are they worried for your safety?"

"What will you do next?"

"Where are you going now?"

They walked as quickly as they could through the town. Chloe hoped that the townspeople would respect her wishes and not follow them, but it was not to be. A good few marched right along behind them. She was sure that they didn't mean them any harm, and were only naturally curious. She said to Onri;

"It looks like we will have to leave as soon as we get back." He affirmed;

"I agree!" In no time they were back to Mr. Carpet, along with the visitors. They positioned themselves and made to depart. Chloe waved to them;

"Thank you for your support, we will come back to visit once we have succeeded!" The small crowd cheered and bade them a safe journey as they incredulously watched Mr. Carpet carry them up over their heads and out over the sea.

"We may as well land on the next island, how about that one?" asked Onri.

"It looks perfect to me, it's uninhabited…ha ha," replied Chloe. Mr. Carpet brought them down, and shortly they found themselves enjoying their supper while gazing out at the setting sun from a high cliff. They all felt tired after their meal and decided a nights rest was in order. They said their 'good nights' and pulled their blankets over themselves right where they were and drifted off to sleep.

Thankfully the night was uneventful. They all awoke around the same time, it was almost sunrise. Chloe decided to try and make some hot cocoa from the chocolate bars that they had left over from Sicily. Before they knew it, they were all drinking hot chocolate and watching a beautiful sunrise over the sea. Chloe said;

"Well, by now the whole world should know our names, and also they should be more certain of what we are trying to accomplish...and that we are not quite using magic. But it may as well be... for, who could understand it, I don't fully myself." They had a nice breakfast from their supplies. It was nice that they didn't have to cook any of it, as it was all cured meats, cheeses, bread and fruit. Onri said;

"We should be arriving at the countries of the middle east after a couple hours of flight... namely Turkey."

"That sounds interesting...okay then, let's get a move on," replied Chloe.

After three hours of flight, the sight of approaching land was welcome to all. Onri pointed;

"If I'm correct, that is either Turkey, or Syria. When they were quite close, Chloe could see the many interesting buildings that made an almost continuous patchwork quilt on the hillsides. Most were small boxy whitewashed stone villas, and dotted quite plentifully here and there were mosques with small minaret towers. Everything had the intriguing look of antiquity.

"Well, this is definitely Turkey, as I can recognize it from photos that I have seen. I hope that we can find a place to land without making a big spectacle of ourselves," said Onri. Chloe then directed;

"Mr. Carpet, please land on that quiet beach near those large rocks, it seems somewhat secluded."

"Why, certainly," he replied. Quite readily they found themselves on the beach in the shadow of those rocks. Mr. Oppum said;

"I think luck has it that we were not seen landing here." Chloe replied;

"Yes, I think you're right...Onri, I am not very knowledgeable of world geography, are we still very far from India?"

"Well, if my memory serves me, the countries that still separate us from it are Syria, then Iran, Iraq, and finally Pakistan. Are we still planning on stopping somewhere before India to wait and see if we can entice Rajeem out of his comfort zone?" Chloe answered;

"Yes, I think that is still a good plan. Maybe the timing and the place will logically present itself to us as we get closer. For now, maybe we should eat a little something, and afterwards you and I could covertly explore a little of the city to learn of Rajeem's influence here."

"Yes, I like the word 'covertly'. It's probably best to stay away from publicity right now. It would only create a problem for us to be recognized and hounded every step of the way." Chloe agreed;

"Yes and its likely better that our enemy does not know of our whereabouts. We don't want to give him the chance to catch us off guard."

After their meal, Chloe and Onri donned hats and sunglasses to better conceal themselves. Chloe also wanted to keep her staff with her as usual, so she slipped a black sock over the jeweled crown of it. Monty said;

"Oh, I should like to come this time. Mightn't I hide in your shirt pocket again?" Chloe answered him;

"You're welcome to come my little friend... hop in." Mr. Oppum waved them off;

"Please be careful, we will keep our guard up here, ta ta." Once in town Chloe noticed that things seemed quite normal ...no jeweled statues, nor the absence of busy city bustling. They then arrived at a crowded bazaar with many labyrinth-like corridors packed with little shops of everything one would or could not know that they wanted. Chloe marveled;

"Oh my, do we dare go get lost in there? I do think the girl in me could shop here for eternity and be happy never to venture out again!" Onri countered;

"Ha ha...very funny, don't worry, you have me to drag you out against your will if it comes to that."

They spent a little time perusing some shops of spices, jewelry, and clothing. Chloe felt entranced by everything that she saw in this foreign place. She then noticed a quaint café on a crowded little corner. There were buckets of flowers for sale on the side walk out front, attended by a small girl with long black hair.

Chloe thought that she looked very pretty while sitting there on her stool. Her cheeks had a natural blush to them, as did her lips. Chloe looked at Onri as they stopped in front of the café and suggested;

"Let us sit at this table and take some tea for a while, shall we?"

"Most certainly, my feet are getting tired." Once they had sat, a man in a white cotton robe and conical shaped red hat came from inside the cafe and asked if they wanted tea. They nodded yes and within moments he had returned with it. He placed it on their little table, along with some containers of cream, honey and sugar. They thanked him as he walked back into his shop.

Chloe was preparing her tea when she noticed that the little flower girl was stealing looks at them. She would look away whenever Chloe returned her gaze. She had pretty brown eyes, and she was dressed in a white cotton dress with bright red embroidered trim.

As Chloe chatted with Onri, it became obvious that they were now the girls' main interest. Chloe wondered if she was an orphan who was forced to sell flowers to get by. After they paid for their tea, Chloe saw that they had only one coin left. She leaned closer towards the girl on the side walk and said to her;

"Excuse me, do you speak English? I wish to buy one of your flowers." The girl answered;

"Yes I do. We are all taught English in school, so you will find that most of the younger people here can speak it." Chloe offered her the coin, replying;

"That's nice, okay I'll take one of the yellow ones." The girl hesitated;

"Your money is no good with me...Chloe." Chloe and Onri looked to each other in surprise. Then Chloe whispered to the girl;

"But how do you know who we are?" She answered;

"Your disguises are good and I did not recognize you at first. But when I kept seeing your friend...Monty is it? ...peeking out of your shirt pocket, I put two and two together. I learned all of your names just today from the latest news reports about when you were in Greece yesterday." Chloe responded;

"Oh...yes, I thought that there wouldn't be much of a delay before the videos were aired on TV that many of the citizens took of us there." The girl continued;

"You will find that you have many, many friends here. And also that they support what you are doing one hundred percent. It is my pleasure, and I am very excited to meet the three of you, my name is Ayla." Chloe offered her hand, saying;

"It is our pleasure as well," as she lightly shook her hand. Ayla rose to her feet and handed her the flower, nervously looking every which way as she did so. She then started speaking in such a low volume, that the three of them had to crane their necks to hear her.

"As I mentioned, you have the support of almost every person in the city, but it is not people that we should be most worried about. There are hundreds of spies everywhere, continuously watching and listening to everything that is said and done. But they are in the form of animals, or ordinary everyday items that you wouldn't expect...like even the chair that you are now sitting upon." None in the party were surprised at this strange news.

Ayla continued;

"If you are finished here, would you please follow me now?"

"Certainly," replied Chloe. Ayla picked up one of her buckets which had no flowers in it, and ducked around the corner of the café. Chloe and Onri quickly sprang to their feet in pursuit, almost toppling over Ayla, as she was only standing right there and waiting. She said in whispers;

"Let us peek at the table where you were just sitting at to see if my suspicions are correct." They all poked their noses around the corner and watched...so far everything seemed still and normal.

Then...unsurprisingly, the legs of each of the chairs began to move. Ayla quickly pulled herself and the others back around the corner, exclaiming quietly;

"We have only moments... they are coming to follow us and will be running around this corner now! You two must grab them, and we will wrestle them around to the back of this café!"

True to her words the chairs immediately came scuttling around the corner with the sound of their wooden legs clacking on the side walk. Ayla muffled in a hushed tone;

"Grab them!" Chloe and Onri each latched onto one, and they were not easy prey as they twisted themselves and kicked with their legs. Ayla motioned for them to follow her as she ran through the alley and disappeared behind the café. They followed her, dragging and wrestling the chairs all the way, which were strong and were kicking them in sensitive areas. They both blurted;

"Ouch!" "Ow!"

They managed to round the corner and stop in a dim corner at the back of the café. Ayla said;

"It is safe to talk back here, as this is my territory. You see; there are no other objects anywhere to be seen near here, as I keep it that way. Onri, I see that you have that blade at your side, would you be able to throw that chair in the corner and quickly disable it before it runs away?" Onri answered as he struggled with it;

"Ugh…Ah…yes, with pleasure!"

He flung the chair over his head with great force and it crashed against a stone wall. But it didn't rest for a moment before it was again scuttling to get away. Onri quickly drew his sword and with a powerful arcing swing, he smashed the chair into a crumpled mass. Ayla instructed;

"Quickly…now disable that one!" Chloe then threw hers as well, and then Onri made a pair of them.

The chairs were not yet dead though, as they were still moving and obviously trying to get away. Ayla said;

"We are lucky that they seem to be newly awakened, for they cannot yet speak. Otherwise they would be making a dangerous racket and calling out for help. I brought this bucket of kerosene to finish them off, as I have done in this place before."

Chloe then noticed that there were indeed blackened ash remains in this very spot. She, Onri and Monty watched as Ayla efficiently splashed kerosene on the chairs, which seemed to realize what was in their cards, for they became frenetic. Ayla continued;

"Okay, stand back." They did just that as they watched her strike a wooden match and throw it onto them. They immediately burst into a not so small bonfire." Ayla added;

"Okay, we only need wait here for a short time as they get consumed." The four of them watched as the chairs stopped moving and were indeed out of commission. Ayla then walked over to a garden hose that was hanging on the rear wall of the café. She turned on the spigot and doused the flames with it, and then turned the water off and rehung the hose. Onri said to Chloe;

"It certainly does seem like she has done this before." Ayla wore a mischievous grin as she smacked her hands together, saying;

"Well that's finished," and went on;

"So what are your plans now...may I ask what you are doing here in the bazaar?" Chloe answered her;

"We came here to get some supplies, mainly some food for our travels. And also to see what were the conditions here as far as Rajeem's influence. We never know when we will learn something new about him, possibly a weakness that we can exploit."

"Ah, that sounds reasonable. Well, I would be happy to help if you would permit me. I have a friend with a shop nearby that will gladly provide you with some food to take with you. Shall I take you to him?"

"That would be wonderful, thank you," replied Chloe. Ayla led them through the back alleys a short distance of only a few twists and turns, and then walked to the front of a little food shop and led them in. It was a quaint, aged shop with barrels here and there filled with dried fruits and nuts. There was a thin middle aged man with short bushy jet black hair and matching mustache standing behind the front counter. When he saw Ayla come in, his dark eyes brightened and he came to the front to greet her. He spoke to her in Turkish, so Chloe did not understand him.

He gave her a warm hug; then Ayla introduced them in English. "Hakan, these are my new friends who you will be surprised to recognize. I give you Chloe, Onri, and Monty." They both removed their hats and sunglasses. The man was truly shocked and did indeed recognize them. He smiled and gasped out loud as he first rushed right past them to close and lock the door. He also pulled down a shade over the window of it.

He then turned around, greeting them;

"Hello Chloe, Onri, and esteemed Monty. I am truly honored to make your acquaintances. Excuse me for slamming the door, but I'm sure that you are aware of all of our spies!" Chloe answered for them;

"It is our pleasure to meet you Hakan; yes Ayla has made us quite aware of the spies..." Ayla interjected;

"Yes, just now after we met in front of the café, we had to destroy two chairs that were onto us... our new friends helped me!" Hakan replied;

"Ah, then you've seen our big problem first hand!" Ayla continued;

"And of course our new friends are here to help; I brought them here because they need some supplies for their cause."

"Then by all means, what I have is yours, please take whatever need!" Chloe and Onri answered;

"Thank you, you are most gracious."

They all busied themselves with filling two medium sized sacks with food and other useful items. When they were finished Hakan said;

"I am very happy to be able to help you, for I know that I am also helping myself, and all the peoples of the world as well… thank you so much for your efforts, and I wish you success!" They all thanked him and exited through the back door. Once in the alley, Ayla asked;

"So will you now go back to rejoin the rest of your party?" Chloe answered in question;

"Yes, maybe you would like to accompany and lead us through these alleys; they seem to be more covert from all of the spies. We would like to go to the beach with the large boulders on its' shore, do you know which one I mean?"

"But of course, follow me." Ayla led them most efficiently through many twists and turns. Suddenly, as they were passing an opening through two buildings, she abruptly stopped and explained;

"Shortly we will be exiting these alleys, but before we do so, you should see what lies just out there…" She crept very cautiously as she led them between the two buildings and stopped just short of entering a square before them. She pointed;

"Please look out there…but don't let your selves be seen by anyone or anything." They obeyed, and peeked out into the square. For the time of day, surprisingly there was not a soul to be seen anywhere. The square was quite large, and curiously almost every inch of the ground was littered with shattered fragments of the crystal. And standing in the midst of it all was a giant white marble statue of their turbaned enemy.

Chloe noticed that on the turban where the jewel would have been mounted, was instead a strange onyx-like black stone. Once Ayla was sure that they had taken in the whole scene, she motioned for them to leave. When they were once again traversing in the relative safety of the alley, she said;

"I will explain later…but here we are at the main highway that leads us to the beach." They then crossed the street and retraced their familiar route back to Mr. Oppum and Mr. Magic Carpet.

Once there, Mr. Oppum was surprised to see their new friend. Chloe introduced them;

"Ayla, this is our friend Mr. Oppum."

"It's my honor to meet you Mr. Oppum," Ayla said, as she knelt and shook his little extended paw.

"Likewise Ayla," replied Mr. Oppum. Ayla looked over at Mr. Carpet and asked;

"Is that your magic carpet? I have always heard tales of them, but never imagined I would actually see a real one!" Chloe answered;

"It is not our magic carpet, but he is Mr. Magic Carpet…" Aylas eyes widened in surprise as Mr. Carpet said;

"Hello Ayla, it's nice to meet you."

"Well hello, I'm sorry about that. I didn't know that you were alive…I'm likewise pleased to meet you as well."

Once the introductions were made, they all busied themselves storing away the supplies that Hakan had given them, and when they had finished Onri asked;

"Ayla, would you please join us for our dinner?"

"Yes, I would be delighted to, thank you," she replied. They all enjoyed the food, the company, and the conversation as well. Chloe thought that Ayla was a very sweet and loveable child, and she could tell everyone else thought so as well. Chloe then asked her;

"Ayla, where are your parents?" Her mood abruptly changed from this question as her eyes became downcast. She was quiet for a spell and seemed overcome by sadness. Then suddenly she began to sob uncontrolledly and buried her face into her hands, as Chloe and Onri exchanged mortified looks. After a couple of minutes, she stopped crying and regained her composure. She said;

"I'm sorry. It's just that I only just recently lost my parents not two weeks ago..." Chloe comforted her;

"My condolences... If it is too difficult to talk about, then you are not expected to." Ayla went on;

"It is painful for me, but I must tell you what happened. A few months ago, after that Rajeem pronounced himself our ruler again, as he once did unsuccessfully before, there appeared that statue in the square. Then, not long after that is when all of the spies began to awaken. Our people very shocked and frightened by this... as it was suddenly such an unimaginable way to have to live. Those horrid things would continuously crawl over to that stupid statue and report all of their suspicions to it. Well, naturally there resulted a large rally in that square which comprised of almost the whole of our city. And as they advanced towards the statue to topple and destroy it, is when the impossible happened. "

"As the crowd pressed in around it, they began to push and rock it off of its foundation. Then suddenly it violently erupted with some violet colored electrical energy, which shocked everyone in contact with it and each other. I was standing a distance away in that alley and watching as this happened to all of my immediate and extended family members who were participating. Then as soon as the energy stopped shocking them, they all fell to the ground. At first I thought all of them may be dead, but after a few minutes everyone had regained their consciousness... but they had become even angrier than they were before."

"Many people had guns, stones, or clubs, which they began using to again assault the statue with. That's when I then saw something... like lightning...emanate from the black stone of the statues' turban. It shot out over the entire crowd, and anyone hit by it immediately transformed into a lifeless purple colored crystal! There were then many screams of terror from all that were still left unaffected. Then to our horror...another volley of lightning again erupted upon them from the statue, but this time it finished killing them, as they all explosively shattered!"

"I watched my entire family, and many friends violently killed in this way...as did everyone else that was there. We all then ran away from the square in terror. And as you saw, no one now goes anywhere near there. But the next day I did go back there. In the dim light of early morning, I crept into the square to the area where I had last seen my family standing. There was nothing discernible to tell which shards of crystal were theirs...but I did find this."

They all watched as Ayla pulled from a concealed place upon her body, a steel dagger. "I immediately recognized my fathers' dagger, which was still in its leather holster. This is all that I have left of them from that day… and I will keep it on my person every day, in the hopes that if I am successful in tracking down that evil man, that I may stab him in the heart with it, as he has in effect done to me…" When she had finished speaking, she was again overcome with grief, and turned her body away from them while still holding the dagger upon her lap. For a time, she stared out at the sea, as the large mellow sun was setting over it.

For a little while, Chloe and company had a quiet conversation about what they had been told. And they decided that they had room for one more to join them. If anyone deserved the chance to hold Rajeem accountable…it was brave little Ayla. As they sat around their camp, Ayla came over to them and asked; "May I sit on Mr. Carpet here, and possibly stay the night with you… if this is where you are staying?" Chloe answered;

"Of course you may, and yes, this is where we are staying for the night. We also have something to ask you… we want to ask you if you'd like to join and help us with what we are doing." Her eyes perked,

"Oh yes… yes…please! I would like nothing better, as I now think of nothing else but tracking down that man and making him pay!" Onri replied;

"Then it is settled then. Tomorrow morning you will leave with us!" Ayla's little face brightened with the news, and she jumped and danced around to give them all her hugs and kisses.

"Oh thank you… thank you, my new little family!" She then looked down at Monty,

"Monty, I have been too shy to ask… but may I hold you?" Monty blushed (as much as a furry faced mouse could) and replied;

"Well… for you I suppose I could allow it…"

Ayla knelt down to him and he let her cradle him in her arms. The sun had set and they were all feeling very sleepy. Chloe distributed their blankets and pillows from their trusty chest and in no time they were all fast asleep, including Ayla with a very comfortable looking Monty still snuggled in her arms.

The next morning when the sun was just beginning to peek over the horizon of the sea on the opposite corner from where it had set, Chloe was the first to lift her head. She giggled when she noticed that Monty had spent the entire night in Ayla's arms, and he did look quite comfortable at that. She got up and busied herself in getting together some breakfast and cocoa for everyone.

Upon hearing her stirring, the rest of the camp arose to help with the chores. As they sat chatting after their breakfast, Chloe offered;

"Well, I suppose with our breakfast now finished, it is time that we get ready to move on from this place." Ayla countered;

"Before we leave, is there any way that we could remove or destroy that cursed statue?" Chloe answered;

"Yes, I have given that some considerable thought since last night, and I am sure that I have the power to destroy it with my staff. But I feel that I should go alone, I see no reason to put any of you in harms' way. I think the most effective way for me to do this is to travel by way of the mist to the immediate rear of it. If I can quickly get to it undetected, and physically touch the jewel upon it, I am sure that will do the trick. I have also conferred in my mind with Mother, and she also agrees this would be the most effective solution."

As Chloe finished relaying to them her plan, she couldn't help but notice that Ayla, as compared to the rest of the party, had the most interested and stern look upon her face. Certainly she had more reason to hate that statue. She asked her;

"Ayla, possibly would you like to go with me to carry this out?" She answered;

"Yes, I certainly would. I feel an over whelming need to see that thing destroyed… yes please take me with you!"

"Okay, then let us go now. Come with me over here just near this rock and away from the others." Ayla walked over and stood next to her. The rest of the camp watched as the two of them stood there side by side.

Ayla felt very apprehensive, as she had no idea what was supposed to be happening. She certainly didn't understand what Chloe had meant by "traveling by way of the mist." Chloe held her staff at arms' length and planted it upon the ground. She said to Ayla;

"I have done this only once before and I don't know if I will be able to speak to you while I'm directing our movements. But from what I remember, we won't feel any physical movement as we go." She then closed her eyes. Ayla stood there looking at the rest of the party and the beach. The first thing that she noticed visually was a wavering… like everything beyond them was being seen through a window of rippled water. Then as described, a violet colored mist quickly enveloped them. She looked up at a concentrating Chloe, and all around them… they were now alone inside of it.

As before when she traveled this way, Chloe found that her movements were being made in her minds' eye. Maybe later on with experience she would be able to see the passing surroundings in real time. But for now, as she continued to fix the location of the statue in her mind, she could feel them getting closer to it. Then, after just a few moments she felt that they were there. With her eyes still closed, she directed the mists to clear away.

Suddenly Ayla was loudly screaming! Chloe opened her eyes... they were in the square behind the statue all right, but they were not alone. Piles of bric-a-brac spies were upon them. Bicycles, chairs, garden hoses... and anything else one could imagine were grabbing and poking at them! Ayla was being pulled this way and that. She screamed; "Chloe... do something quickly!"

Chloe was also being violently grappled by all of the junk, but she was very near the statue. She struggled to free her arms and legs from them. She didn't dare let go of her staff, which was also an intense focus of the spies' energies. But she certainly was still holding onto it and in control of its powers. She willed the plasma to radiate forth, which it did... surrounding her in a violet colored corona. Any spies touching it immediately went limp, but Ayla was being carried away screaming.

Chloe kicked and pushed away the piles of dead spies, and made her way to the front of the statue. The onslaught didn't abate even for a moment, but it was now useless for them. Chloe stood before the statue and quickly raised her staffs' jewel to the onyx stone of its turban and gave it a light tap. There was the sound of a quick thunderous crack that echoed around the square, followed by the sounds of all the now inanimate spies falling to the ground where they stood. Chloe looked back and saw Ayla at the edge of the square, pulling herself from atop a pile of them.

Ayla made her way over to Chloe and stood with her as they surveyed the once chaotic scene. The square was a complete littered mess. There was a bottom layer of sad, shattered crystal. And above it all, covering every inch were the dead spies. Ayla exclaimed; "Thank you so much, you did it Chloe!"

"Yes, we did it! I'm sorry about the surprise entrance for us here…"

"That is certainly okay…just look at the results!" Ayla then looked at the cursed statue,

"I hate that thing…" she said, as she walked over to it. She kicked it and then started pushing on it to try and topple it over. Chloe joined her in pushing on it. They managed to get it rocking back and forth… and then slowly as it passed its' apex, it toppled backwards. They jumped back away from it as it loudly crashed to the ground atop the dead spies, cracking and splintering into fragments. They watched the dust settle; then Chloe said;

"Okay, our deed is done. Its' best we leave now before the square fills with revelers." They looked around and it was still quite deserted… except for one lone person standing at that same alley. Chloe could see that a man was video recording them on his smart phone, she wondered how long he had been recording them. She said;

"Okay, let's go." The mist once again enfolded them and in no time they were back at the camp and relaying to the others what had transpired. Onri congratulated them and added "Well, I had no doubt about the outcome. I've gained complete confidence in you Chloe… you are one truly amazing girl."

Ayla walked over to where Monty was sitting on Mr. Carpet and sat next to him. He didn't have to ask her what she wanted, so he just hopped up into her arms. Chloe watched with some amusement as it was obvious that a love affair was in their midst. Mr. Carpet asked;

"Well, what is now the consensus of where we should go to next?" Onri offered;

"The next country that we will traverse would be Iraq. If we are able to stay aloft for a few hours, we may be able to pass it by and land in the country of Iran... or Persia as it is preferably called my most of its' people. Mr. Carpet... you are a Persian carpet are you not?"

"I am indeed, and that is where I was made... by hand. Although I don't have any memory of being there, as I was not an aware being at that time." Mr. Oppum asked him;

"Did you not land there for a night during your journey to America?"

"No, we were quite desperate to travel as quickly as we could then, but I would be most interested to stop there this time." Chloe added;

"Then lets' try to make it to Persia in one move if we can." As they were already packed and ready to go, they were again aloft in just a few minutes. Ayla whooped with joy as she reveled in her unimaginable flight upon a magic Persian carpet.

Chapter 11

Ethan and Rowena were sitting in the brush of some far off place…they didn't even know where, near some ugly, boring, and dusty little village. There were spent piles of canned beans littered around them and they were yet once again enjoying another one. Presently, it smelled a little gassy around there as Rowena angrily threw her unfinished can at a tree trunk which splattered sloppily on it… and onto Ethan as well. He yelled testily;

"Hey…knock it off! Now I got sticky beans all over me!" Equally testy, Rowena countered;

"Aw shut your trap. I'm sick of it here… and I'm sick of beans…beans…beans… and I'm sick of you too!" Whenever they snuck into the village to pilfer something to eat, they only ever found the same thing…beans.

Rowena continued to look over at Ethan. His feathers had grown back…but they were still sitting here in this stupid place, waiting for their next instructions. Rowena said;

"Why haven't we heard from Master? All we do is sit here and wait. If we don't hear from him soon we must conclude that he has given up on us since our last defeat. We should just leave this place. I can't take it here any longer!"

No sooner had Rowena finished speaking when their masters' eye appeared on Ethan's' necklace. It said;

"No, I haven't given up on you. Yes, it has been some time since we last spoke. Our enemies are still on the move and getting nearer to me as we speak. I don't yet have any specific plan for you, but to be prudent maybe it is time for you to intercept their next resting place. It will probably be a full days' flight for you to be where that may be, so whenever you are ready, all you need do is travel in an easterly direction and I will fill you in as you go."

"Thank you Master..." they both quipped eagerly. The eye then vanished from the shard. They both looked at one another and then wasted no time in leaving that hated place.

Chloe watched with a little sadness as they left behind the jewel of the Mediterranean. And as the hours went by, they passed over a spectacularly beautiful Iraq with its' ancient cities of golden mosques and its' rolling desert dunes which were interspersed with caravans of camels and elaborate tented encampments. At one point as they flew over a large city, which must have been Baghdad, they saw planted in the center of a large and empty square another one of Rajeems cursed sentinels. Only this one was gigantic...and certainly more menacing looking.

They took care to widely circumvent it and to stay out of its' line of sight. It was getting late in the day towards dusk when Mr. Carpet said;

"Well folks, I'm pretty sure we are now passing over the border and into Persia." Chloe added;

"We definitely should be careful in trying not to be seen by anyone as we approach and land. We must suspect that spies are everywhere."

In no time there was a very large city coming into view. Ayla said;

"That would be Tehran, and yes we should be very cautious of spies and land very soon, before we are seen." They landed in a large grove of palm trees, along a thin creek. Everyone arose and hopped off of Mr. Carpet to stretch their travel wearied limbs.

It was getting past dusk now, so this would obviously be where they would be spending the night. Everyone helped in their chores of preparing a simple meal, and afterwards they found themselves in good spirits while conversing and lounging around their dark camp. Mr. Oppum said;

"It is a dark and moonless night, and it is certainly prudent to not light a fire here for fear of attracting attention. If its' any comfort to anyone, I can see perfectly well in the dark and will notice anything nearby that moves...and I will be awake for hours, so everyone get a good nights' sleep." Onri countered;

"Thank you. That is a very nice relief for us...I'm exhausted, good night all." They all said good night and plopped down onto their blankets and pillows. It was a quiet nights' sleep, as not even a breeze blew the entire time.

The next morning they all awoke with the sunrise feeling very rested and refreshed. Ayla sat with Monty amongst her rumpled blanket and announced;

"I'm still full from dinner last night. I don't want anything to eat this morning." Monty also agreed;

"Yeah, me neither." Everyone else also expressed the same. Then Chloe interjected;

"Well, since our plan is still basically unformed, other than trying to coax Rajeem away from his strong hold to some place, and we don't yet know where that location would be… maybe we should again venture into the city to gather some insight. Also, I was thinking that this would be a perfect opportunity to get Mr. Carpets' singed off corner repaired, since this is the land where he was made. There are probably scores of carpet weaving shops nearby." Onri agreed;

"Yes, good idea…I'm for that." Ayla also added;

"Luckily, I speak a little Persian, as I am also a Muslim and have had some Persian friends. We are also lucky as well that it is somewhat customary for women here to wear a full burka if they choose to. I have heard that everyone here is extremely suspicious of foreigners, so if we can get a hold of three burkas, I'm sure that no one in town would give us even a glance as we walked along while wearing them and carrying a carpet to be repaired." Chloe said;

"That sounds perfectly logical, but how in the world do you propose getting them?" Ayla answered;

"I think it should be easy for me if I go to the nearest mosque and tell them a little fib. I will tell the Imam that I need to borrow three burkas for myself, my mother, and my auntie, so that we can come for morning prayers. I bet he would loan them to me if they have any spares lying around." It wasn't long before Aylas' plan worked perfectly and Chloe, Onri, and Ayla were walking down a dusty road towards town carrying a rolled up Mr. Carpet between them.

It was hot, stifling, and hard to see well from the slit in the black burkas they wore, but the anonymity they provided was worth their weight in gold. It wasn't long before they were in the midst of the city. And sure enough, no one gave them any mind as they trudged along with the carpet...they may as well have been invisible.

They spoke to each other only when they were not in earshot of anyone. Ayla was in the lead in case anyone actually spoke to them. Then without fail they came upon their first carpet shop. Ayla stopped them in their tracks as soon as she noticed it. She said to them;

"Well what do you know; a carpet shop in Persia...Imagine that!" Onri chuckled,

"Okay, ha ha very funny..." Ayla said;

"Okay, let's wander in and see what happens." They entered in single file carrying the carpet and went straight up to a man standing there among piles of carpets for sale. Chloe was surprised at Aylas command of the language... she had obviously been modest about her fluency. Their conversation went back and forth for a couple of minutes.

The man then obviously wanted to see the carpet in more detail, so Ayla began to set it down. Once it was partially rolled out, the man pointed to a marking in one of the corners and continued talking about it for another minute. Then it seemed that the conversation was over as Ayla obviously thanked him for his time and bowed her head.

They again rolled up Mr. Carpet and walked back outside and down the street a little ways. Ayla then stopped to tell them what he had said.

"He said that he recognized the maker of this carpet and that we may as well go there, as it is actually not too far from here." Mr. Carpet shuddered with glee as they held onto him and said;

"Oh my, I never thought I would be going to where I was made. This is somewhat exciting for me, although I don't really know why...ha ha!" They all laughed, as it was indeed kind of funny.

Ayla led them per the mans' instructions, and within ten minutes they were standing in front of a quite elaborate shop in an obviously higher rent district. Ayla said;

"I'm certain this is it...it is exactly how it was described." She led them through the open doors. Again as before, they walked straight up to a man standing next to a very tall pile of carpets. Although this time there were two men. Chloe thought they looked like brothers. They both stopped talking when they noticed them standing there.

Ayla spoke to them in Persian, explaining that they wanted to get the carpet repaired, and that his competitor down the street had said this carpet was made here. She was directed to set it down and roll it out completely, as there was ample room to do so. They set it down and all three of them stood at its' end and evenly walked upon it as they unfurled it.

Once they were done, they turned around to see what the men would have to say about it. Chloe thought that she saw a momentary look of recognition on the men's faces, but it was fleeting. They started speaking to Ayla in a relaxed, nonchalant manner. Chloe and Onri hardly noticed that the other man had walked over to the front door.

But when it loudly slammed...accompanied by the sound of a heavy dead bolt being thrown, they all looked and saw the brother standing there and pointing a gun at them! He ducked behind a tall stack of carpets, but still had his gun trained on them as he peered around it.

They looked back to the first man, and he too was ducking behind a stack and pointing a gun. They then shouted in Persian and English in unison.

"Do not move and take off those burkas immediately, or we will shoot you where you stand right now!" Certainly they meant business, so they all three ripped off their garments. Chloe was careful to try and keep her staff concealed inside the folds as she held onto it.

The men then spoke in turn;

"We know who you are."

"And believe us, we don't enjoy doing this."

"Of course we recognize the carpet, as it is one that we made especially for Emperor Rajeem."

"And the one we have been watching you fly around with on the television." Chloe asked;

"But why, if you don't want to harm us, are you holding us at gunpoint? Don't you want to be freed, along with the rest of the world from him?" They again answered in turn;

"That is exactly our dilemma...of course no one here in Iran wants to be ruled by Rajeem."

"But since he took over, he has completely neutralized our fanatical government."

"We could hardly believe it when suddenly we were free of them and all of their restrictions."

"We are even able now to travel outside of our country and return whenever we want."

"There is no way that we will go back to the way things were before."

"So you see, we don't want to harm you...but we will NOT let you leave!" The brothers began rapidly speaking to each other in Persian. When Ayla heard what they were saying, she quickly translated it in a whisper to Chloe;

"They are about to shoot us in our legs..." Chloe whispered to them;

"When I give the word, drop to the floor and hold onto our Mr. Carpets' rope here…Mr. Carpet, get ready to take us out of here." Chloe then said aloud as she revealed her staff from the folds of her burka;

"Then I'm sorry to disappoint you gentlemen…GOOD BYE!" Simultaneously they all dropped to the floor as Chloe pointed her staff at the front doors. An intensely bright violet flash then blew them off of their hinges and sent them hurtling out into the street, immediately followed by the four of them as they flew through the smoke. Alarmingly, they also heard gunshots exploding and whizzing past their ears. Within seconds they took stock and saw that they were unharmed and safely flying away from the city.

When they got back to Monty and Mr. Oppum, they only had to have them hop on and they were ready to go. Ayla then said;

"Before we leave here, do you mind if we circle back to that mosque to return these? I would always feel regret if I did not give them back." She revealed the two crumpled burkas that she was still holding onto. Chloe, still clutching hers, answered;

"Of course we can Ayla, just lead us there." Ayla pointed the way, and as they flew by the high window of the mosques' turret, she tossed all three of them into it.

As they flew away to the east, they wouldn't have noticed their two weary pursuers just arriving in their wake. As they landed at the now abandoned camp Rowena said to Ethan;

"Well, there they go… we made good time traveling here, but we desperately need a rest." They then both literally fell over backwards in exhaustion and didn't move for hours.

Onri relayed to Monty and Mr. Oppum the events in the city. Chloe added;

"Yes, that was all very much unexpected… but alas here we still are, all safe and sound. Ayla, where do you think we will be after flying in this direction for a few hours?" She answered;

"I should think we would be near or in the country of Pakistan, which would be the last one before India," and then queried;

"Yes, I am sure that's correct. Is that where we are planning to stay while finalizing our strategy?" Chloe answered her;

"Yes, but we should try to find someplace where there is not a large population… I think we would be distracted by too much attention." Ayla then offered;

"Well, if we can make it to edge of Pakistan on the border to India… in the mountainous region of Kashmir, I should think it may serve our purpose." Onri also concurred;

"Yes that could possibly do…" Chloe replied;

"I have heard of Kashmir, and being in the mountains away from everything may be what we are looking for. Mr. Carpet, do you know the way there?"

"Yes Chloe, I remember it. I will have us there in a few hours."

Once they finally made it to Kashmir, they spent some additional time in the air to find a suitable place for mounting their defense. Onri said;

"I should think that being on a small hill with some cover by trees would be better than being trapped in a gully or valley." Ayla then pointed to a medium sized rocky hill. It was really more of a small mountain with many large boulders on all of its sides. Chloe said;

"Yes I think that may be a good location for us. There doesn't look to be any way to traverse to its summit very easily by foot. Mr. Carpet, please take us there." They landed in a small clearing near some trees. They then all wandered to the edge of a cliff which overlooked a spectacularly rugged view of many snowcapped mountains. Mr. Oppum offered;

"I should think that it gets very cold here in the winter, thank goodness it is now still late summer time." Onri added;

"I would like to do some exploring of our little mountain to see what natural defenses it may have." They found that its' summit which they were on was a good size in that it wasn't large enough for an enemy to easily conceal themselves there without being detected. Also, without much searching they found a large cave which would be perfect for them to live inside comfortably. It even had separate rooms which had 'windows' that looked out in different directions.

In no time they had themselves set up in their new home. And like children, they had excitedly staked out and claimed their favorite bedrooms. They all had fun entertaining themselves by playing house… meagerly decorating their rooms with their bedding, spreading Mr. Carpet onto their "living room" floor, and setting pinecones and pretty rocks they had found onto imagined mantles and shelves. Chloe thought it was nice to just be a child again for a little while, she missed playing. It seemed they all felt that way, for they spent the whole afternoon playing inside and outside of their wonderful cave.

After the sun had set, and they were all comfortably lounging inside after their supper, their conversations turned to the pressing matter at hand for which they were all there. Onri stated;

"We are lucky to have found this cave. It seems we could be quite comfortable here for as long as we need to stay." Chloe agreed;

"Yes, actually I am relishing the prospect of spending some time here while plotting and carrying out our plans." Ayla joined in;

"So, what do we think will be our course of action while staying here for this duration?" Chloe answered;

"Our plan was to draw Rajeem out of the protections that he would have on his own turf. But to do that we will need to do more than just wait here. We will need to foray into areas near here and disrupt his control of them. I should think that after a campaign of doing this over a period of time, it would cause him to have to act... probably first by setting his emissaries upon us, and then ultimately if that failed him, he would have to attend to us personally." Ayla countered;

"That really does sound logical...I would have to say..."

Rowena and Ethan awoke from their naps after a few hours. They had no new information from their master about where exactly they should again try to track the enemy. Rowena said;

"I don't know if it was just dumb luck on our part that we were on their trail before, but all I suppose we can do for now is just to continue on our present course in an easterly direction." She hopped onto Ethan's' back, and after a running start they were again aloft and in pursuit.

After an uneventful but otherwise very comfortable nights' sleep in their new home, they all wandered outside to sit at the cliff after their breakfast. Chloe said;

"Well, as usual we will again need to find some supplies. There is at least a source of water nearby." They all looked down to the base of their mountain at the creek that was flowing past it. It was there that they all noticed the dirt road that crossed it. They hadn't seen any town nearby from the direction which they had come yesterday. But the dirt road did show some promise as it continued onwards. Ayla said;

"Maybe that road leads to the next town. Should we follow it?" Monty hopped into her arms, almost startling her as he said;

"Yes, let us all go!" Chloe answered;

"Yeah, lets' go..."

They then all stepped onto Mr. Carpet and off they went. As they flew off, they just missed the arrival of their pursuers.

Rowena and Ethan saw the departing company and took this perfect opportunity to see what they had been up to. In just a few minutes they discovered their comfortably furnished cave, and as they picked over the breakfast leftovers that were left out, Rowena said;

"Hmmm... it does look as if they are planning to stay here awhile. Just then their masters' eye appeared on Ethan's' necklace and said;

"Well done my pets... you have succeeded in informing me of their whereabouts. For now you will find someplace nearby which will suit you comfortably as well. We will wait to see what those idiots are planning." They bowed to the eye as it disappeared,

"Yes master."

The party came upon a town somewhat quickly in a small valley. It seemed very primitive, as all of the buildings and dwellings were made of clay mud bricks. And the people who were not walking were going about in crude donkey drawn carts. Onri said;

"I suppose we have found what we were looking for, shall we go down there?" Chloe answered;

"Yes…but there certainly is no reason to hide any longer. Mr. Carpet, please take us to the center of town. But we must be on our guard from the start, as we have no idea whether they are friend or foe." As they landed right in the middle of the town, it was no surprise that they caused quite a stir. Some people ran away in fear, others stood dumbfounded. And still others did indeed recognize them and came running up to them to introduce themselves.

The first men to arrive said;

"Hello Chloe and company, my name is Jafar, and this is my friend Shakir. We are honored to meet all of you!" Onri answered him;

"Hello Jafar and Shakir, it is our honor as well." Chloe then interjected;

"Hello and greetings…we're not a little apprehensive to land directly here…do we have spies and enemies to worry about here in this town?" Shakir answered laughingly;

"Yes, but that is nothing new for Kashmir. This place has been in conflict for generations. The neighboring country of India has always been at war with us to claim ownership of this place." Jafar added;

"But yes, things are different now. We have new enemies and new spies since the second coming of Rajeem. We have fought with him and sadly…we have lost. His spying statue is standing at the other edge of our town just down there." They both pointed behind themselves.

Chloe then said to them;

"We have come here to continue our cause…the liberation of the world from him. We are planning on staying here near your town for some time if need be. Right now we are camped on the top of the smaller of your mountains just back from where we came. This road passes by it, as does a small stream. Do you know of which place I'm speaking?" Jafar answered for them;

"Yes, we certainly do. There is a large cave up there that we played in as young boys." Onri replied;

"Yes, that is where we are staying…and if you should need us at any time you will find us there." Chloe then said to them;

"You said that his statue is at the other end of this town, maybe we will take a walk there right now…" Chloe and Onri began walking with their new friends, followed by Ayla, Monty, and Mr. Oppum as they remained seated on a floating Mr. Carpet. A growing crowd was following them as they walked.

Ayla asked them;

"You said that you have fought with Rajeem, have you lost many of your people here in that fighting?" Jafar answered;

"Sadly…yes. It is now mostly very quiet here these days. And no one goes near the statue, so that part of town is always deserted." As they walked along, it was indeed noticeable that they were entering an unused part of town.

In fact it was completely devoid of anyone, and the small businesses were vacant if not partially destroyed. It was also sadly apparent that they were seeing and stepping over a thickening mass of shattered crystal shards as they went. Shakir said;

"Maybe we should stop for a moment… there it is." They stopped and looked as he pointed it out. Chloe could indeed see it standing off to the side of the dirt road. It was about two more blocks away.

Just then, there was a disturbance from one of the vacant shops… a noise of falling debris. Then out crawled a spy. Oddly, it was an old fashioned sort of spinning wheel for making thread. It stopped once it was in plain view and just stood there observing them for a minute or two. There was much murmuring from the crowd just behind them.

Chloe got a chill down her spine as they stood and watched that evil thing just standing there…then with some clacking of its wooden legs on the ground; it quickly scuttled away towards the sentinel. When it got there, it stood right next to it…seemingly conferring with it. Jafar then said to them;

"Having an assembly of our people out here near the statue is something that is never done now. In the past it has only provoked a deadly response from it. We are far enough away from the statue right now to be out of its range to harm us. But the mist can form anywhere to wreak vengeance upon us, though usually there is time for us to disperse and run away before it is fully formed."

Suddenly there were many more sounds coming from the vacant buildings, and varying forms of spies began piling out. Chloe heard many gasps of concern coming from the crowd behind her. She looked back towards them and saw that they looked ready to flee… she turned to Shakir and Jafar and said;

"Would you please ask them not to flee… and that we are here to help. I would like to make a show of defense right now, and I can offer some protection." Jafar quickly spoke to them and they seemed willing to comply, as none of them moved away. Chloe then said to them;

"I alone will advance towards the statue, as I'm confident that it cannot harm me. But you all will have to defend yourselves from the spies if they attack you here. When I make it to the statue, I will be able to disable it and all of its spies. You only need to hold out against them for this short time. We will let Rajeem witness this through his sentinel... okay, here we go." Onri and Ayla pulled out their weapons and stood their ground. The crowd also brandished, either what they had on them already, or could grab nearby.

The area ahead of Chloe became chocked with the spies, and they just kept multiplying. She held her staff out before her and released its protective corona, which surrounded her body, and began advancing forward.

The hoard immediately swarmed around her, and also towards her company with the crowd behind her. Just as before, the spies fell away lifelessly as they came into contact with the staffs' energy. But the rest of her friends had to fend for themselves' against the onslaught. Chloe's' advance was slowed by the sheer amount of the dead bric-a-brac she had to circumvent, or climb past, to get to the sentinel. She looked back periodically to see how the others were doing... and began to worry that they were beginning to get overwhelmed.

She saw Onri, Ayla, and all the others valiantly holding their own while swinging their weapons and smashing the spies to bits...but she needed to speed up her advance a little. After climbing over the last pile, she finally made it to the statue... when suddenly the air around it became electrically charged, as the onyx stone of the turban began emanating its own protective corona around the entirety of itself.

This time, Chloe found it impossible to physically come into contact with it, and when their coronas touched, there was a violent eruption of blinding and shocking energy, and she had to back away. She looked back at her friends and was alarmed to see that they were now overwhelmed, and possibly being harmed...she had to act fast to end this now!

She again faced the glowing sentinel...and raised her staff towards it. A violent charge of plasma shot forth towards the onyx stone, which also released its own charge. The two opposing streams of energy collided in a shower of sparks and earsplitting cracks...but neither hers' nor the statues stream wavered in acquiescence.

There seemed to be a stalemate... she needed to somehow add an advantage. As she watched the two streams' violent and opposing immobility, she looked to the right side of the statue. It was close to a hillside...and there were many heavy boulders poised above it. She didn't know if this would work, but she held out her free hand towards them... and willed some of her jewels energy to follow this additional trajectory.

It certainly did work. She watched as another stream of plasma shot towards and struck the boulders. A thunderous explosion rocked the hillside, and immediately the large boulder... along with a few other ones... tumbled noisily downwards toward the sentinel. They struck it perfectly and shattered it. Immediately the energy from it ceased as it was now only a pile of rubble. Chloe looked back and saw her friends and the crowd standing amongst all of the now lifeless junk. As they saw her looking their way, a loud cheer arose as they all excitedly jumped up and down while waving their arms, then hugging one another in jubilant celebration.

When she got back to her friends, she was hoisted atop the crowd in a show of excitement and appreciation. She let them handle her and pass her along as she also reveled in their success. Finally, after a good few minutes of cheering and dancing in the street, she was set back down to stand on her own. Jafar and Shakir were there with their family members, and they thanked them as they passed along some rations of food and drink to take with them back to their camp. Chloe said to them as she and her friends made themselves ready to depart on Mr. Carpet;

"Thank you all as well for the supplies. I'm glad that you all may be a little safer in your homes tonight, but unfortunately we all know that we have not yet won our battle. And as we've said before…we're not yet leaving this place. We will now go back to our mountain camp, and if you need us, that is where we will be. Good night all!" They all waved goodbye to the crowd from atop Mr. Carpet as they rose above them and flew off towards their mountain.

Rowena and Ethan were still on the mountain when Chloe and her company returned. They watched from a concealed spot high up in the branches of a tall pine tree as Mr. Carpet landed near the mouth of their cave. After they all disembarked and disappeared inside, Rowena said;

"I wonder what those dummies have been up to…" Ethan replied;

"Hadn't we better go find some shelter of our own someplace as master has told us to?" Rowena looked around them,

"I think this is going to be all that we can realistically find in the area. To leave this mountain would not afford us the ability to keep an eye on them, and finding some place on the ground here would leave us open to being discovered by them... yes, this spot is comfortable and safe enough for us, as this is a very wide branch and I could easily sleep upon it."

Once inside their comfy home, Chloe, Onri, Ayla, Monty, and Mr. Oppum enjoyed their meal which they had set out upon their make shift table, the travel chest. A bottle of wine was also given them and they were being very grown up as they shared it while celebrating their latest victory over Rajeem. Ayla asked everyone;

"I'm so happy to be able to help anywhere people need it. When I think of my poor mother and fathers' defeat in our square back home, I get so sad...and angrily determined to make Rajeem personally pay for what he has done to me and everyone else. How long do we think we will have to wait here to draw him out?" Onri looked at Chloe and then answered;

"I suppose there is no way to know that, but I might venture to say that it won't be very long... as we are so close to his home now, and he may be getting very impatient from his failed attempts at getting rid of us."

No one noticed that hiding near, and spying into one of their windows at them, were their most reviled foes. And the eye was also present and listening from Ethan's' necklace. As the early evening progressed, there were gathering clouds in the dusky sky outside. Chloe began to hear some thunder booming not so far off, but didn't make any worry of it as she continued chatting with her dear friends.

Then, suddenly they all heard a thin screaming voice coming from somewhere outside. They all looked at one another, jumped to their feet in alarm, and ran outside to see where it was coming from. They heard it again and ran to the edge of the cliff to look down. Someone was midway up to them, climbing with perilous abandon. Chloe said;

"It looks like either Shakir or Jafar." When he saw them looking over the edge at him, he stopped climbing and funneled his hands to his mouth and again yelled to them;

"It's me...Shakir. Please help us; our town is being destroyed by the eye!" They all looked up and saw that something was indeed brewing in the skies beyond the mountain that was in between them and the town. There was a thick blanket of dark, red-black clouds visible...and frequent flashes of what must have been lightning lighting up the dusky sky.

Chloe yelled down to him;

"Shakir...don't move, I will be right down to get you!" She had her staff with her and Mr. Carpet was at her side, so she was ready to help immediately. She inquired as she stepped onto Mr. Carpet; "Would everyone please wait here...except Onri, could you accompany me?"

"Of course," he said, as he also jumped on.

The others watched as the pair swiftly swooped down to pick up Shakir and then fly off towards the maelstrom. Shakir then told them; "About an hour ago the eye appeared, along with an angry and awful storm. It was immediately apparent that it was hell bent on destroying our town and everyone within it as it unleashed much furious lightning...from the clouds, and more devastatingly from itself as well."

"I immediately ran here to alert you…I'm very afraid to see what or who is now destroyed back home." When they rounded the mountain top, the scene in front of them was pure chaos. Thick roiling clouds, the color of black coagulated blood, were unrelentingly pummeling lightning at any structure or person on the ground that was not already dead or burning. And horrifyingly, the giant eye was prominently peering down from a dark magenta mist. As it looked to and fro, a chillingly sinister laugh could be heard echoing from it…as it also pelted its targets with bursts of red plasma. The three of them gasped at the grisly sight.

Mr. Carpet stopped their advance and held steady…awaiting instructions. Shakir began crying;

"Oh my god, all of my family and friends…I'm afraid they may all be dead." Chloe said;

"We haven't a moment to spare; if there is anyone left to save we must act now! I will attack the eye with the power of my staff, but I'm afraid that I may possibly only come to a stalemate, as he also has the same powers. I will part with you here to make my stand…and if you can, try to stay near and unnoticed to wait for a chance to strike him as well. Unfortunately, even if we defeat him here, this is only but a battle which would probably still leave him safely in power at his real location…luck be with us!"

Onri and Shakir watched as Chloe extended both her arms outwards while her right one tightly gripped her staff. And as her head tilted back slightly, a crimson radiation erupted from the jewel and ensconced her in its corona as she ascended into the sky towards the eye. Mr. Carpet quickly backed away as to hopefully keep them unnoticed. As the crimson haloed form of Chloe neared the horror, it ceased its laughter and downwards attacks as its chilling gaze swung to look at her.

The sheer size of it was maddeningly intimidating, and became more so as it scrutinized and squinted in its' hated concentration of her. As Chloe came as near to it as she dared, she saw its' surrounding magenta colored mists abruptly darken to a deep purple. And its' violet colored iris, which also matched hers, began to brighten in intensity. Chloe changed her stance.

She slightly crossed her lower legs, pulled back and raised her free left arm to arc upwards, and extended her right to aim the staff. Simultaneous bursts of crimson plasma blindingly illuminated the now dark evening sky and entire area as they struck in cataclysmic opposition.

Anyone still left alive from the previous attacks below to witness it would also be enduring a painful, deafening explosion that rocked the ground to the core. As the initial fission diminished in intensity; the two adversaries could still be seen…locked in an ebb and flow of what must have been an excruciatingly painful and fatiguing trading of energy.

Onri and Shakir watched in astounded fascination. Onri exclaimed;

"I don't know how much more of that Chloe or anyone could endure…Mr. Carpet please take us as close as you can!"

"Yes sir," he replied, as they immediately sped towards the event. Onri again requested of Mr. Carpet;

"As fast a speed as you can muster please Mr. Carpet, pray we get some element of surprise to help save our own skins as well... hold on Shakir!" Mr. Carpet gave it his all and tripled their speed as Onri unsheathed his sword. Their velocity stretched their skin and whipped their hair as they came at a perpendicular angle to it.

Chloe watched as they approached the energy spewing eye. And as they reached within an arms' length to it, she saw Onri take a sweeping aim and fling his sword at it with all his might as they made an about face and sped away.

Onris sword glinted with a bright reflection as it traveled the short distance and penetrated the unearthly flesh. There came from it a tremendous echoing shriek of pain as it ceased in its' attack. The energy spewing from it died away, and blood could be seen pouring forth from a gaping wound. Chloe continued to direct her jewels surging energy at it until it suddenly vanished. As it did she saw Onri's sword fall to the ground, followed by her friends in pursuit of it.

She followed them, and once on the ground, they all hugged one another to acknowledge their victory and survival. Shakir said to them;

"Thank you my friends...but this is still a very sad day for me...I will leave you now to go home...hopefully to find my family still alive." When they had said their good byes, Chloe felt the welcome feeling of Mother invading her thoughts...she said to Chloe;

"It appears we may be near to the event which we have sought... I am sure that the jewel which we seek is now at your mountain cave..." Chloe turned to Onri with a look of complete surprise and shock, which startled him. He asked;

"Chloe...what is it!?"

"Mother has just informed me that Rajeem is now at our cave!"

As Ayla, Monty, and Mr. Oppum waited apprehensively inside their cave; they could only imagine what perils their friends faced out there, and what the outcome would be. As the three of them sat around the chest, Mr. Oppum said;

"I am so nervous and afraid for them, I feel that I am going mad... what do you suppose is happening?" Ayla answered him;

"I just don't know...after that frightful scream...and then the dark quietness afterwards over there...I just..." Ayla stopped speaking in midsentence as they all jumped with a frightful start. The dreaded mist was forming at the entrance of their cave.

None of them felt that they had any way of defending themselves as they ran into the next room. While peeking around the corner, they watched as the mists faded away to reveal the evil man himself. He was wearing his traditional royal Indian garb of purple satin robes, matching curled and pointed shoes, and a purple satin turban, which was expectedly adorned with the misused jewel.

But there was one obvious and unexpected feature upon him. Both his eyes were missing within empty black sockets, which were trailing blood...he was blind! Although he certainly did not look defenseless as he was surrounded by a violet colored corona of energy.

Just then, Monty and Mr. Oppum were shocked to see their old nemesis scamper into the room to greet him...Rowena! And with her was that frightful crystal necklace wearing eagle who helped her attack them once before. They stood before their master, looking up at him. Rajeem said to them;

"All is not completely well...I am now visually impaired...but not completely blind, as I can still use my powers to see. That little brat Chloe and her stupid friends will be here momentarily...I detect their approach. All of these other little turds must be killed immediately, are any of them here now?" Rowena answered him;

"Yes, three of them are hiding just there around the corner." Rajeem commanded them;

"Get them…Kill them now!" Aylas eyes widened in terror as she looked at her friends hiding there with her. The three of them then scattered to find places to hide as Rowena and Ethan bounded into the room. Ayla had found a small crevasse behind a boulder in which she jumped, but her friends had been spotted. Rowena purred; "There you are my old friends…are you ready to die tonight? Get them!" Monty and Mr. Oppum ran from them, made it to the window and hopped outside, followed by their pursuers.

Outside in the dark, Monty and Mr. Oppum ran towards the cliff, for they knew there was a route down the mountain side from there if they needed it. Monty looked over his shoulder as he ran and saw Ethan's familiar talons almost again gripping him from above… he dove onto the lower platform of the cliffs' shelf just in time as Ethan swooped over and missed him. Mr. Oppum was also at Montys' side as they both jumped onto the shelf, with Rowena stealthily springing just after them.

Chloe, Onri and Mr. Carpet raced back towards the cave, and when they arrived they flew directly inside to confront Rajeem. There was no particular plan of attack… this was it. Chloe thought either she would win or she would lose, but she would try her best. When they passed the entrance of the cave, he was standing there… alone and waiting. He looked of a surreal nightmare, surrounded by a pulsating violet corona of energy. Chloe and Onri jumped from Mr. Carpet. Onri backed away as he unsheathed his sword and crouched, ready to spring to his death if need be.

Chloe stood her ground before him with her staff at the ready...which emitted her own encircling shield of a corona. It was only then that she became fully aware of the past and present damage to his eyes which she had inflicted upon him. But she knew that he would not be completely blind, as she herself had before used the power of the jewel to see while in the mist.

Rajeem then said to her; "You have caused me much pain and trouble, you filthy little wretch...and now it is time for you to pay...prepare now for your certain death!" Chloe did not get a chance to respond verbally to him, as he immediately began attacking her.

He cupped both his hands before him and massaged from the air a sphere of pulsating energy, the full power of the jewel then shot forth towards her. Chloe pointed her staff and she also unleashed its power. As before, the two streams of energy met with an overwhelming cataclysm of fury.

Onri felt himself being blown back by the force of the explosion and hitting the cave wall. He lost his grip on his sword as it clattered away, and as he crumpled to the ground he felt himself lose consciousness.

Ayla could see everything from where she hid through the passageway as she crouched behind the safety of a boulder. She was thankful to be shielded and still conscious immediately after the explosion. There was still much smoke...and she couldn't see what was happening. She pulled her fathers' dagger from its leather holster under her shirt where she always kept it...the time was near for its true purpose.

As Chloe stood there, she could not believe the force of the resultant explosion...and being inside the cave had made the sound all the more deafening. She now heard little else than some loud ringing in her ears. Also it was surprising that any of them could have survived it.

But here she was, still standing within the protection of her corona. As her eyes adjusted back to normal after the blinding flash, and the smoke cleared a little more, she saw that yes, Rajeem was still there as unharmed as she was and directing his energy against hers. She glanced over her shoulder and saw poor Onri crumpled on the ground.

She felt panic…the pain of the sustained onslaught became shockingly apparent and was excruciating to every nerve in her body. Her stamina was rapidly waning and her legs were getting wobbly. As hard as she tried to keep herself erect upon her feet…she could not. She sank to her knees. Her arms suddenly felt very heavy… just keeping the staff pointed in his direction was beginning to seem a feat.

She stared at his face…that evil face…he grimaced a white toothed smile from that black beard and it was all that she could now see. It was mouthing words…and they were invading her mind. Like far off whispers which were gaining in volume. Echoing and bouncing to and fro inside her head. So loud now as to drive her mad, she realized it was only one word in a raspy whisper which was repeating and overlapping upon itself and making her dizzy; "die… die… die… DIE!!!"

Monty and Mr. Oppum landed from their jump onto the shelf of the cliff, with Rowena on their immediate tail. As Monty scurried away into a hole behind a rock along the wall, he watched with a feeling of helplessness as Rowena pounced on Mr. Oppum. She certainly meant to go for his throat as she missed her mark and sank her teeth into his lower neck and shoulder area.

Mr. Oppum screamed in pain as Rowena locked her jaws on him and started using her lower clawed feet in trying to disembowel him. But an opossum is not a defenseless creature, in fact they are quite formidable and terrifying to behold when cornered and infuriated. He bared his teeth to her, which were larger and sharper than hers, and sank them into her throat. Rowena screamed her cattish wail and let go of his shoulder.

Just then, Monty's view was obscured, as Ethan was now directly in front of him at the opening of the hole which he was watching from. Monty flung himself backwards just in time to avoid the beak that was pecking... pecking...trying to stab and grab him. Ethan pushed his head farther inside the hole, snapping...pecking. Monty felt his back against the wall...there was no more room left to retreat.

Mr. Oppum now had Rowena locked into his jaws. He had her by the throat, and the taste of her warm, salty blood was now pervading his mouth. Frenzied by the bloodletting, he shook her to and fro unmercifully, and as she continued to scream her death song, he flung her with all his might over the cliff and into the darkened void. Her screams could be heard trailing off until they were gone forever.

Mr. Oppum looked over and saw that eagle pull his head out of a hole, from where he was most certainly attacking his friend. He ran over to help, as luckily, the eagle must've decided to give up...for he just flew away. An exhausted and panting Monty emerged from the hole and happily hugged his friend, saying;

"Mr. Oppum, are they really gone? Oh thank heaven!" They then both ran back towards the cave. There was some diminishing smoke coming from its' entrance, and they could also see the energy flashes of the battle through it, so when they got there, they decided it was safer for them to enter through the 'window'. They hopped up onto its sill and witnessed the perilous scene in shock and wonderment.

Ayla now saw her chance to avenge her parents, and to help Chloe and the world as well. But there wasn't much time. Chloe looked as if she was almost finished, and Onri...poor Onri, she couldn't tell whether he was alive or dead. She suddenly felt a sense of complete selflessness pervade her being. She thought that she may very well die in her attempt at killing him, but was absolutely steeled to the purpose.

She saw that along the wall of the cave to his right, there was a fissure in the floor that she could crawl along while staying concealed, and that it ended at a large rock which was just in front and off to the side of him which was about the height of his chest. She gripped her steel dagger more tightly in her hand and wasted no time in crawling as fast as she could over to the rock.

Onri was having a very realistic dream...it involved their final battle with Rajeem. And as he was taking part in it, he started hearing a very loud droning inside his head. This seeming reality then faded away when he opened his eyes...but the droning was still there. Where and when was he? He now saw a rock floor where he lay. He was just only dreaming? It seemed so real...he blinked his eyes and lifted his head. His grogginess quickly began to fade as he realized what was really happening.

He saw Chloe upon her knees, fighting for her life as Rajeems jewel plasma stream was erasing her ...and he saw Monty and Mr. Oppum standing in the window watching in horror! Where was his sword? From where he lay he looked around himself...but it was nowhere to be seen. Then he noticed that there was some movement over at the cave wall to the left of Rajeem...

Ayla had made it to the rock without being detected. She could still see Chloe from where she was, and the situation was grave. She thought of her mother and father...gone because of this man. He had killed them and everyone in the square that day with no more thought than stamping an insignificant anthill.

Well, not one of the hundreds or thousands of people he has killed in the past year has been insignificant, she thought. And my mummy and dada were my most special love. She screamed within her mind; "I love you mummy and dada!" With tears streaming down her cheeks, she jumped to stand atop the rock...she paused there only momentarily to gain her balance and to raise and aim the dagger. With a shrill and piercing scream of bloody vengeance, she leaped off of the rock onto him and sank the razor sharp dagger to the hilt straight into Rajeems heart.

Ayla fell to the ground and backed away hurriedly on her posterior. Rajeem screamed in mortal pain as his attack upon Chloe ceased and he staggered backwards, hitting and leaning against the wall. "NO!" he screamed, as he realized that he was surely dying, and that his rule was certainly over.

A look of pure hatred flashed across his face as he looked down at Ayla, and with his last gasps of breath and strength, he managed two last feats of evil. He first directed a beam from the jewel of his turban to strike Ayla, which turned her to crystal, and secondly he grabbed the hilt of the dagger…managed to pull it from his chest…and flung it straight at her, shattering her into a thousand bits of glass.

As Rajeem fell dead onto the floor of the cave, the whole company screamed as they watched poor little Aylas death; "NOOOOO!" As near to death as Chloe was, she forgot all of her own pain and fatigue when she saw little Aylas body shatter.

She dropped her staff and crawled over to Aylas remains…there was nothing there to even hold or caress…she felt completely heartbroken and crushed. As everyone else also converged on the spot, they all sat among the pieces of her…hugging one another and sobbing uncontrolledly. Chloe choked through her sobs;

"Ayla…Ayla…brave little Ayla…she saved us all!" There was nothing else to be said that could bring her back or extinguish their most overwhelming grief, so they all sat and mourned her there for quite some time.

Chapter 12

The next morning after a very long and dreamless nights' sleep, Chloe chose the somber task for herself of gathering together the broken pieces of Aylas remains. It was so far the most difficult chore of her young life, and she was sure that it would always remain so. She put them into a burlap satchel, which originally housed the bottle of wine that was given them.

As she did this, Onri went over and removed Mothers' jewel from the turban, which had fallen from Rajeem's head and bounced a short distance away as he fell dead. He was thankful for this, for he felt as the others did…that this evil man deserved not even one thought or glance in his direction.

And that is how they treated his remains…completely forgotten and left to rot where it lay. It was well after midmorning when they gathered themselves outside around the chest to have a little something to eat. Monty exclaimed;

"I can hardly believe it…we did it!" Onri added;

"Yes, we certainly did. I think a group high five is in order!" He then raised his palm low over the table and they all high fived one another while cheering; "YAY!" Chloe then added;

"Thank you all so much, and I thank Ayla as well...may she rest in blessed peace...we were a true team and still are. I think also that we are now friends for life, as we may be soon spending the rest of our days on this earth together in seclusion with Mother from the coming disruptive events described by her." Onri then offered;

"Yes, all of us living together in that wondrous place does seem quite surreal, but it is a probable outcome. I wonder if the world community is aware today of any changes...some things must be different..." Mr. Oppum replied;

"Yes, at least all of the spies must be gone." Chloe countered;

"I wish we were near a television, it would at least help us to shape our plans for further informing the media and the world as to where we go from here. I really do not relish the thought of dumping the bad news upon the world concerning Mothers' plans for the future of fossil and nuclear fuels. But first things first, I would like today to leave this place and travel back to Ayla's town to see her friend Hakan, so that we may tell him and her people of her bravery and sacrifice."

After a little while they again had everything packed and secured onto Mr. Carpet, and when they were all seated and ready to go, Chloe gave the word;

"Ok, Mr. Carpet if you please...you know the way." Chloe thought, as they took to the air, "My, what a feeling of relief I have this time as we're flying off to our next destination. No more feelings of anxiety over facing unknown dangers."

They first decided to fly over the mountain village on their way out to see how it was fairing. As they saw, it was pretty much completely destroyed. But there were signs of hope as the survivors were bustling around to clear the rubble. When they got a little closer, a cheer could be heard as the villagers waved to them. Onri pointed downwards; "Look, there is Shakir and Jafar." They were all glad to see that the two of them were alive and well, as they waved goodbye to them.

After two days travel, they made it to Ayla's home town in Turkey. As they flew over the square, they saw it was bustling with activity. Gone was the rubble of the sentinel, the dead spies, and the copious crystal remains that had littered the ground. Their presence didn't go unnoticed for even a moment though, as they passed overhead.

They were greeted with excited cheers as everyone in the square pointed, waved, and shouted greetings. Chloe waved back smiling. She said to Mr. Carpet;

"Will you please take us to the alley behind Hakan's shop; we will land and see if he is there." Once they were on the ground, Chloe decided to ask Mr. Carpet to stay out of sight and not create a stir, and wait on the roof as the rest of them went around to the front door. Once inside they found Hakan standing behind his front counter.

When he saw them, he smiled and excitedly came over to greet and hug them all. It was apparent that he was looking from face to face to find Ayla, and when he saw that she was not there, he queried in his tongue for her. They must have all had sad looks upon their faces, as his then mirrored theirs. After holding up his finger to suggest that they wait for a moment, he darted out the front door and then returned promptly with a woman in tow. He then closed the front door and spoke to her. She listened, and then turned to them and said in English;

"Hello, I am very happy to meet all of you, my name is Melda. Hakan has asked me to speak with you, since he thinks that his English isn't so strong. Let me first say how grateful I and everyone here in this city are to you for helping us. And secondly, Hakan has asked; where is our little Ayla?"

Before answering her directly, Chloe explained that she needed to have a public record of events going forward and asked her if she happened to have a smart phone. They were in luck as Melda pulled one out of her dress pocket and held it up with a smile.

Chloe and the rest of them then took turns telling their tale of defeating Rajeem, and of Ayla's brave part in it…as well as her sad demise. There were many tears shed from them all as the accounting was told and the satchel and dagger were given to them. When they had finished, Melda took Chloe aside and politely asked her about her attire, and that if she needed any, they could go to her clothing shop next door and choose a few things for her. Chloe looked down at the worn out and singed rags that she was wearing. She certainly did need some new clothes, she thought.

After she changed into a new, flattering light green cotton dress, and some brown leather sandals, Chloe thanked her and Hakan for everything, and explained that it was time for them all to go. As they all said goodbye, Chloe also asked if they could please upload the video onto the internet that Melda had taken, so the world would hear of the events, and of Aylas bravery. They answered that they would immediately, and bade them farewell.

Once back in the air on Mr. Carpet, they discussed their next destination. Chloe said;

"Well, I suppose Onri that the next place on our list would be to your parents' home in France, as it is next in our path." He answered;

"Yes, I really miss them. When I last spoke to them in Paris, they said that upon my return, I would find them back in our village where you and I first met." And that is exactly where they went. Chloe had them land in the same field as before. She thought that strangely, it seemed almost a lifetime ago that they were here, but it was just that so many things had happened since. Chloe gave Onri a big hug to say good bye, and immediately following, they shared a tender little kiss upon the lips.

Chloe felt sparks, and as their eyes locked after embracing, it became evident that they had developed strong and lasting feelings for one another. Chloe's mind raced in longing to already return here to him, even though she had not yet left…she excitedly imagined a life together soon in their coming seclusion.

She could tell that Onri was also thinking the same as she said; "We will be back here soon I suppose, to collect you on our way back to Mother…I hope that you will still want to go with me there." Onri blushed;

"Nothing could pry me from you now Chloe. Should I ask my parents if they want to come as well?"

"Yes, that should still be the plan that Mother has suggested…to bring our loved ones there to live with us. Ok, until then…goodbye for now my Onri"

"And goodbye to you my Chloe…and also to you Monty, Mr. Oppum, and Mr. Magic Carpet." He then stepped onto the grass and waved them goodbye as he watched them rise and slowly fly away.

When Chloe and her friends finally completed their return voyage across the Atlantic Ocean and arrived at the shores of the United States, Chloe said to Mr. Carpet;

"I've given it some thought, and have come to the conclusion that the monumental news that I must deliver to the world is just that...too big. We must find our way to Washington D.C. and talk to our president at the White House." So, without too much trouble, they found it and proceeded to land directly on its front lawn. As expected, there was much ado from a security standpoint, but she was quickly recognized and welcomed inside to talk to the president.

After she had revealed to him everything that was told to her by Mother, he thanked her for making the right decision to let him determine when and how to relay the news to the world. Chloe could tell that he did believe what Mother had told her by the grave look upon his face, but told her that he would have to wait before making any statements until there was proof of what she had said was true, and that he would have their scientists keep a vigilant watch over any molecular changes of those elements should they occur.

He thanked her again as they walked back out to the front lawn of the White House. Chloe wasn't surprised by the media attention that had assembled there as she shook the presidents' hand. There were scores of reporters with news cameras that were chomping at the bit to gain access to her, but thankfully they were held back by security.

As Chloe and her friends departed and were flying over the long gates which bordered the street, it was again apparent how fast word of their presence had travelled, as hundreds or more people were cheering them. They were shouting their thanks and waving hastily made signs which said; "We love you" and "Way to go Chloe!" among others. They waved back as they flew off...and marveled still as they saw almost the whole city had come to a standstill and was watching and also waving their departure.

It took another days' travel before they were finally nearing her Grandma Jens house. Chloe was hoping that there would not be a camp of media trucks to spoil her return. And to her great relief, as they cleared the treetops that bordered the house, she saw that all was as quiet and peaceful as they had left it.

As they flew directly into the open French doors of the attic, she noticed that her Aunt Meg and Uncle Jim's car was parked on the driveway, as they were surely awaiting her return. She said; "Oh boy, am I in trouble...ha ha...I'm afraid!" They all laughed uncontrolledly, as they spilled rolling onto the floor of the attic together in a fun jumble.

Chloe then heard a commotion of voices and advancing footsteps from her family as they burst into the room. They hugged and kissed her welcome. Grandma Jen exclaimed;

"Chloe...I just can't believe it's you...it's been so long!" And her Auntie Meg laughingly said;

"I don't know whether to scold you or praise you...ha ha...you put us through hell with worry!" Uncle Jim also added;

"But when we watched the amazing progress of your quest and travels on TV, we became less worried at least...but now you're here, you're really here...and it was all real...I can't believe it!" Chloe answered them with more hugs and kisses, saying;

"It's good to be back, I've missed you all...I'm sorry if I worried you."

Her family then went downstairs to the kitchen for some celebratory cake and ice cream. Chloe told them that she would be there to join them in a few minutes, and when they had left, the room again erupted in celebration. Piano played music, and there was much rejoicing for both their reunion and their triumph. Chloe then said to them when things quieted down;

"And now you all should have no more fears of losing your wonderful consciousness…oh yes, I almost forgot that there was one of your friends here that I never got the chance to meet." They all looked over to the lifeless grandfather clock.

Chloe retrieved her staff from where it was resting on the floor and lightly tapped the clock with its jewel, which produced a mellow, glowing flash. She said;

"There, that should do it. I suppose after a little time we shall have your friend back with us." She turned to Monty and Mr. Oppum and said;

"Lets' go have some well-deserved cake and ice cream shall we?" Monty smacked hip lips;

"What are we waiting for…lets' go!" and they immediately tore downstairs.

Chloe spent some wonderfully relaxing weeks at her Grandma Jens house. Having breakfast every morning with her Grams, playing with all of her friends in the attic, and outside with Monty and Mr. Oppum as well. She used this time also for informing her family of the upcoming catastrophic events described by Mother, and the offer of sanctuary for them all. As incredible as this news was to them, they sadly accepted its' truth, as they had no justification for disbelieving her.

Then, one particular evening when Chloe was lying in bed and drifting off to sleep, the warm milk of Mothers words entered her mind.

"My little Chloe…are you still awake?" She thought back;

"Yes Mother, it is good to hear from you. I've been thinking lately that it was time for me to contact you…to ask when you will be making the changes."

"Yes, that is why I am now contacting you. The fact is, today is the very day in which I have done this with your permission." Chloe sat up in her bed…the news was not unanticipated…but it was still very sobering. She replied;

"Mother...at least four of us will be returning there shortly...I just thought that you should know."

"Yes, I thought that would be so, also there is one more thing that I wanted to tell you before you came here."

"...Yes?"

"I have told you before that I exist as a collective of consciousness from the combination of all life here on the planet."

"Yes, I remember."

"Well, it is also true that the theology of what you would call reincarnation is, to a certain extent, a valid one. When the living matter of something dies, its consciousness...or memory...does not. The DNA that was within that life...which placed it on its' own particular plane of consciousness...gets physically reconstituted back into its next, new type of DNA through the natural recycling process of matter, it still carries a harmonic echo of its' past memories, which can be directly accessed. It could be called; evolutional cross genetic memory."

"I call it harmonic because all DNA has a specific number of chromosomes, and when a particular DNA strand loses its living matter and gets reconstituted back into whatever new form of DNA is next, its' memories will carry over into the new form to a certain extent. That extent is contingent upon the harmonic number of chromosomes present in the new form as compared to that of the last. A harmonic would be defined as an even multiple in the number of chromosomes which would affect the resonance...or transfer of information between them. The strongest retained memories would occur if the new DNA type was exact...such as from human and then back to human again. But the further away from likeness or harmonic multiple it is to the next form would be the measure to which these memories fade."

"Fascinating…" Chloe marveled.

Mother went on; "I know from being in contact with you… all of the particulars of your families' DNA. And I can tell you that I know the exact present location of the reconstituted life forms of your mother and father." Chloe actually fell out of her bed and hit the floor with a thump. Her head then popped up over the side of the bed as she knelt there on the floor. She queried;

"Do you mean that I can again see and talk to both my mommy and my daddy!?"

"Yes, that is exactly what I mean."

"What form has their DNA been reconstituted into?"

"They must have been together when they perished…with their bodies remaining untouched for some time, for they are now both in the form of Steel Head Trout. And oddly enough they still remain emotionally tied to one another, as they are even now swimming side by side in a small river… in where you would call Northern California."

"Fish…my parents are now fish? And since they are not human, their memories will be degraded to a certain degree as you have explained…but by how much?"

"The DNA between animals which share commonalities, such as skeletal vertebrae's, are really not so far apart from one another. Now, if their next form was a tree for example, it would not be possible to access enough memory to speak to them. But since they are now fish, I should think that most of their memories would be accessible after a rather simple realignment of their brain synapses, which you can cause to effect."

"Can we go to see them now!?"

"I understand that you are anxious to see them now, but it would be easier to accomplish all of what you would want to by the light of day."

"What do you mean by all of what I would want to accomplish?"

"Well, you would not only want to see them, but you would also like to retrieve and take them with you as well, would you not?"

"Yes, you are right…I certainly would!"

"Then let us wait until the morning at least. We will speak again when you are ready to go, good night Chloe."

"Thank you, and goodnight Mother."

Needless to say, Chloe didn't sleep a wink all night. She was of course beside herself and counting every minute. And when the sun did finally peek over the trees, she was already sitting in the kitchen and waiting for Grandma Jen to come and join her for the breakfast that she had made for them.…she had to find something to do, it may as well have been that.

As she continued to drum her fingers on the table while waiting, she finally heard her Grams coming down the stairs. When she rounded the corner and saw Chloe waiting there she said;

"Oh my goodness, what have we here? You made breakfast for us? Did I forget it's my birthday or something?" Chloe answered;

"No, but I just wanted to have a special morning for us, that's all." Chloe didn't want to relay to her yet all of what Mother had told her…she would let the news of her parents' reincarnation be a surprise for a later time. While they were chatting and enjoying their pancakes, her Grams asked;

"Are you sure there is no special occasion?" Chloe answered;

"Well yes, I suppose there is an occasion here. Last night I was informed by the earth spirit, whom I told you about, that she had enacted the changes to the worlds' energy supply yesterday. So I've decided that today I will be going to the sanctuary after first checking to see if Onri and his family members are ready to join me there. I feel that probably only Onri will be ready to go, and that his parents will choose to wait for a while."

"I imagine that you probably would also like to wait until a later time as well, is that true?" Grams answered her;

"Oh my, I will miss you terribly when you are gone. But yes, you are right. I am not ready to leave here yet." Chloe then said to her;

"It is no trouble for me to come back here at any time, as the method of travel provided for us by the spirit is comfortably quick…even though the distance is great. I've enjoyed our breakfast together, and now I will go up and pack." Chloe hugged and kissed her Grams, and then went up to her room. She didn't have much to pack, and was finished fairly quickly.

As she stood in front of the vanity table mirror, she admired the green dress that Melda had given her in Turkey. She found that her tastes had changed, as she now preferred to wear this, and the other dresses she received from her, over her slightly tom boyish attire of before. They were pretty and they now suited her, she thought. Her hair had grown out a little and she looked a bit more mature. Also the dresses reminded her of her beloved little Ayla, who she would never see again.

She opened the drawer of the vanity and pulled out the larger jewel that the nameless one had used. Before Onri had given it to her, he had spent a little time incorporating it onto the brass buckle of a thin brown leather belt that he had. She fashioned it around her waist and looked at it in the mirror. She thought that it looked quite pretty with her dress.

She went down stairs to say good bye to her Grandma Jen, and told her that she would come back soon to check on her. Then she went back upstairs, retrieved her suitcase from her room, and continued on up to the attic. Everyone was there as if waiting for her. Monty and Mr. Oppum wished her a good morning when they saw her come in and set down her suit case. Monty said;

"I did happen to see you packing this morning when I wandered by your door early this morning..." She offered;

"Yes, I am leaving this morning to go to Mother's sanctuary. Are you two ready to go today as well?" Mr. Oppum answered;

"Am I ready for another adventure? You bet!"

"Me Too!" chimed Monty as well. Just then, Chloe was contacted by Mother;

"Hello Chloe, are you ready to go?"

"Yes, the three of us are going to leave here now, are you going to be able to direct me to where we're going first?"

"Yes."

Chloe turned to the rest of her friends and said;

"There is one more thing I need to do before we go." She went to the open French doors and picked up her staff, which was resting against one of them. She then pulled the jewel free from it and said;

"This one we will keep here to ensure some continuity of life for all of you here," and went to her new friend, Grandfather Clock, and opened his front cabinet, continuing;

"Good morning Mr. Grandfather Clock, would you mind keeping this safe in here?" He answered;

"Good morning Chloe…of course not, and I should think we will never again let it out of our sight!"

"Good," she said, as she hid it inside of him. She then picked up her suitcase and stepped over to the open French doors and turned around. Monty and Mr. Oppum then joined her by standing upon either side of her. As they faced their friends for a farewell, Chloe said to them all;

"My dear friends…what a wonderful and fantastic adventure we have all had together. Brave Mr. Magic Carpet, you first helped to create our family up here by rescuing my Grandfather and safely bringing him back here so long ago. And to all the rest of you, I want to thank you as well for being my special friends. For inspiring and believing in me…a freckle faced little girl with messy red hair…who'd ever have believed, besides you, that I could go out and save the world. Until we soon meet again… farewell."

Piano started playing one of his favorite lively little tunes as they all shouted their goodbyes. Monty, Mr. Oppum, and Chloe waved goodbye as the amethyst mist appeared, swiftly enveloped them, and then vanished with them.

As the three of them stood motionless inside the space folding mists, Chloe had a private conversation in her mind with Mother. "Mother, I can feel you guiding me to our destination. How long before we are there…my nerves are completely rattled with anticipation."

"Then you can now calm down, because you are already there and can safely exit now." Chloe directed their mists to evaporate, and as she expected, they were standing outside in the bright morning sun amongst some mountains somewhere and next to a slow moving stream. She immediately walked to the edge of the stream with her suitcase, set it down, and began scanning the waters before her for the two fish that Mother had said were there.

After a few moments, she realized that they were directly in front of her, seemingly motionless in their swimming against the mild current. The color of their bodies was very similar to that of the stream bottom, and after adjusting her vision to see past the camouflage, she could see that they were not small fish, and very impressive indeed. Mother asked;

"Did you bring a container with you?"

"Yes, here it is" she said, as she took it out of her suitcase and set it onto the ground.

"What should I do now?"

"You should be able to direct the mists to envelope them and transport them into the container...I will do it for you if you feel that you can't."

"I feel confident that I can do it...here goes." Chloe closed her eyes and placed her left fingers lightly upon the jewel at her waist. And when she felt the task was done, she opened her eyes and there they were in the container. They looked a little cramped in there but they were not yet too agitated. Mother went on;

"Chloe, you should awaken them now, so that they won't struggle and quickly use up their oxygen in there. They won't immediately remember you or themselves for a few hours yet, but they will have vastly more intelligence right away and become more docile. Also, if your journey takes too long, you will have to take a break to find them replacement fresh water." Chloe agreed;

"Ok, we won't delay even for a moment."

She again closed her eyes and fingered the jewel. She searched for the minds of the fish, and immediately found them. They seemed to have multiple compartmentalized stacks of recessed memories... with a type of barrier between each.

She was surprised at how easy it was for her to see this, now that she knew what to look for. She willed the synapses of their brains to make pathways to their next stacks. Chloe opened her eyes and studied them floating there in the glass container as they looked back at her. She then said to Monty and Mr. Oppum; "Ok guys, I have awakened the reincarnations of my parents, and now we must hurry on with our travels."

She again willed the mists to envelope them, and after a few minutes of folding the space between them and France, she cleared them. Mr. Oppum exclaimed in exasperation;

"Wow that was so fast. Here we are in that same field!" Chloe then looked to her right, and to her surprise, there was Onri sitting there upon the low rock wall along the road. He jumped up in surprise, exclaiming;

"Chloe...Monty...and Mr. Oppum!" He ran over to Chloe and hugged her, saying;

"My Chloe, I've come here every day since you left. I wanted to take no chance on missing you, you're all that I've thought about…I love you Chloe!" Chloe felt her heart completely explode upon hearing those rapturous words from him. She said;

"My Onri, you're also all that I've thought about!" They stood and swam in one another's eyes for a moment, and then they shared the most romantic kiss that Chloe thought could never again be matched. When they parted, Onri took her hand and looked down curiously at the fish within the large glass bowl with a bewildered look upon his face. Chloe said with a mischievous smile;

"Onri, I'd like you to meet my mother and father." He burst out laughing at the seeming joke and looked up at her…but she looked serious.

"Huh…?" he said. Chloe then burst out laughing at the preposterousness of it, replying;

"Ha ha…the look on your face! But it's true… thanks to Mother, I've been reunited with the actual reincarnations of them, and am awaiting their memories to awaken if you can believe it!" He said;

"These days…I can believe anything."

Chloe then said to him;

"We must be on our way to Mothers' sanctuary as soon as possible…do you need to go to your home to get your belongings?"

"No, I have my bag just over there. Lately I've been anticipating our actual departure. My parents are planning on coming at a later time if things get unbearable here. But just a moment, I promised them that I would tie this green ribbon on a tree branch over here if I had left with you, so that they would know when I left." After Onri tied on the ribbon, he picked up his suitcase which he had sitting there below the branch, and stepped back over to them.

"Ok, now I'm ready," he said, as he stood next to her.

The mists again enveloped and folded them, and within a few moments the four of them found themselves once again in that wondrous flower filled land of the volcano. Chloe looked off into the distance and saw the eternal flame of it. Everything still looked exactly as beautiful and perfect as it was before.

Suddenly, they all became giddy as Monty and Mr. Oppum then spied the fruit trees. Monty exclaimed;

"There are those delicious fruit trees again…come on, lets' go!" and off they went. Chloe looked down at her parents in the bowl, and said;

"Onri, come along with me, let's put them into the lake."

"All right," he answered, as he picked up the Bowl and let her lead the way. When they parted the fragrant foliage, they found the lake was also as beautiful and pristine as they had left it. Onri handed her the bowl.

"Here you are my love."

"Thank you…my love," she said in return, as they smiled at one another. She took the bowl from him and they walked over to the lake. She knelt, and gently poured the water and fish into it, then sat upon the black sand to watch them.

Onri sat next to her and put his arm around her shoulder as the fish quickly darted away into the depths of the lake. Chloe then said;

"Onri, I do believe that we will be happy here together." He looked deeply into her eyes and replied;

"I do as well my Chloe." They again shared a romantic kiss. Then, suddenly they heard a splashing sound, and looked to see both of the fish were in quite shallow water, facing and looking at them. Chloe held her breath…then one of them stuck its head above the surface and said;

"Hello my little spunky."

THE END

ABOUT THE AUTHOR

Jerry J Yeaman was raised and resides in the San Fernando Valley of Los Angeles California. He holds degrees in electronics engineering and the culinary arts. In his earlier years he collected and read comic books as well as novels of science fiction. He loves animals and currently has a small rescue terrier mix dog named Chloe. This is his first novel and attempt at writing. He was born January 3, 1964

www.ingramcontent.com/pod-product-compliance
Lightning Source LLC
Chambersburg PA
CBHW070836120626
46556CB00002B/777